THIS IS LOVE

Barbara Cartland

Barbara Cartland Ebooks Ltd

This edition © 2020

Copyright Cartland Promotions 1997

Book design by M-Y Books
m-ybooks.co.uk

THE BARBARA CARTLAND ETERNAL COLLECTION

The Barbara Cartland Eternal Collection is the unique opportunity to collect all five hundred of the timeless beautiful romantic novels written by the world's most celebrated and enduring romantic author.

Named the Eternal Collection because Barbara's inspiring stories of pure love, just the same as love itself, the books will be published on the internet at the rate of four titles per month until all five hundred are available.

The Eternal Collection, classic pure romance available worldwide for all time .

THE LATE DAME BARBARA CARTLAND

Barbara Cartland, who sadly died in May 2000 at the grand age of ninety eight, remains one of the world's most famous romantic novelists. With worldwide sales of over one billion, her outstanding 723 books have been translated into thirty six different languages, to be enjoyed by readers of romance globally.

Writing her first book 'Jigsaw' at the age of 21, Barbara became an immediate bestseller. Building upon this initial success, she wrote continuously throughout her life, producing bestsellers for an astonishing 76 years. In addition to Barbara Cartland's legion of fans in the UK and across Europe, her books have always been immensely popular in the USA. In 1976 she achieved the unprecedented feat of having books at numbers 1 & 2 in the prestigious B. Dalton Bookseller bestsellers list.

Although she is often referred to as the 'Queen of Romance', Barbara Cartland also wrote several historical biographies, six autobiographies and numerous theatrical plays as well as books on life, love, health and cookery. Becoming one of Britain's most popular media personalities and dressed in her trademark pink, Barbara spoke on radio and television about social and political issues, as well as making many public appearances.

In 1991 she became a Dame of the Order of the British Empire for her contribution to literature and her work for humanitarian and charitable causes.

Known for her glamour, style, and vitality Barbara Cartland became a legend in her own lifetime. Best remembered for her wonderful romantic novels and loved by millions of readers worldwide, her books remain treasured for their heroic heroes, plucky heroines and traditional values. But above all, it was Barbara Cartland's overriding belief in the positive power of love to help, heal and improve the quality of life for everyone that made her truly unique.

AUTHOR'S NOTE

The Master of the Horse is esteemed as the third great Officer at Court, giving place only to the Lord Steward and the Lord Chamberlain of the Royal Household.

Formerly this Officer was called 'Constable, and held much more power than his successors of today.

He now has the charge of ordering and disposing of all matters relating to the Sovereign stables, races and breeds of horses and has jurisdiction over the Equerries, Pages and many others employed in his department.

At State Processions he rides next to the Sovereign and, in the case of a Queen Regnant, in the carriage with Her Majesty.

At the Coronation of Queen Victoria the Master of the Horse and the Mistress of the Robes rode in the State carriage with the Queen.

The present Master is the Duke of Westmoreland.

Historically records of the appointment started in 1391 with the first Master of the Horse, Sir John Russell.

There were four previous holders of the position starting in 1360, but Sir John Russell was the first to hold the title officially.

He served King Richard II faithfully.

CHAPTER ONE
1885

Lady Athina Ling turned her horses off the main road and drove down a narrow lane.

She resented having to slacken their pace because it was growing late and she was still a long way from home.

The hedges were high and so she drove ahead with considerable care.

At the first bend of the lane, however, she was forced hastily to pull sharply at the reins as to the front of her and coming out of a field was a farm wagon.

The wagon's horse was right across the lane and the farm yokel driving it realised somewhat belatedly that there was other traffic on the road besides himself.

He managed to turn his horse as Lady Athina was pulling in hers as hard as she could.

The chaise would just have had room to pass the farm wagon if the wagon had been pointing straight up the lane.

As it was, the lighter wheel of the chaise then crashed against that of the wagon.

The horses came to a standstill and the groom with Lady Athina jumped out.

The wheels were fortunately not locked together as they might easily have been.

But at the same time the wheel of the chaise, being the lighter of the two, was somewhat damaged.

"You was a-comin' along too fast!" the yokel said aggressively, fearing that someone would blame him for what had happened.

"I am afraid I was," Lady Athina replied in a soft voice, "and this lane is very narrow."

"Folks've said that afore," the yokel remarked.

Her groom came to the side of the chaise to report,

"I'm afraid, my Lady, the wheel's been damaged. Not badly, but it'd be a mistake to try and get 'ome on it."

"You mean we must have it mended first?" Lady Athina asked. "If we can find someone to do it."

The yokel was listening to their conversation.

"There be a blacksmith up at *The Crown and Feathers*," he said, "and 'e be good 'un, if 'e ain't gorn 'ome."

"And where is *The Crown and Feathers*?" Lady Athina enquired.

He pointed down the lane that she had just come along.

"It be down thar," he said, "'tis the best Posting inn in these parts and it be on the left."

"Thank you," Lady Athina replied, "now please tell me where I can turn."

He indicated ahead and the groom jumped into the chaise. Very carefully, Lady Athina tooled her two well-bred horses to where there was a wide entrance into a field. She then carefully turned the chaise round.

As they drove back past the farm wagon, the wheel of the chaise was bumping and felt somewhat unsteady.

"You are quite right, Gauntlet," she said. "We could not reach home with it like this."

"I'm afraid it'll take a good hour to mend, my Lady," Gauntlet replied.

"Well, if it does, we will just have to stay the night at the Posting inn."

There was then a poignant silence and Lady Athina knew that he disapproved of the idea.

Gauntlet had been with her father since she was a child and now that he had died, Gauntlet looked after her almost possessively as if she was one of his own children.

"It's no use being disapproving," she said after a moment when he did not speak. "I know that I should have a chaperone, but then you are far more effective than even Mrs. Beckwith could be."

"People'd be shocked, my Lady, if they knowed you was a-stayin' in a public inn without Mrs. Beckwith in attendance."

Athina laughed and it was a very pretty sound.

"You are making me seem as if I was Royalty, Gauntlet! It will be only for one night and, if you think it might cause a scandal, I will not use my own name."

She paused before she added,

"I will be 'Mrs. Beckwith' – and why not?"

Gauntlet made a strange sound that signified neither approval nor disapproval.

As she drove on, Athina thought just how lucky she was to have him with her.

She could always rely on him in an emergency and, if there were drunken young men at the inn who insulted or tried to be familiar with her, Gauntlet would deal with them.

The wheel was decidedly more wobbly by the time *The Crown and Feathers* came into view.

It was indeed, as the yokel had informed her, a large impressive Posting inn for such a sparsely inhabited part of the country.

Lady Athina was aware that there were no stately houses nearby where she might have found friends.

However, to have gone back to where she had come from would have been almost as far as going home.

She had been staying the night with an ancient aunt who had been on the verge of death for the last five years.

Athina was quite certain that she would last for at least another five before she finally arrived at the Heaven that she was convinced was waiting for her.

In the meantime she enjoyed more or less compelling her relatives to visit her.

When they arrived she tantalised them with promises of benefiting from her will and such promises were usually rescinded almost before they left.

As far as Athina herself was concerned, she wanted nothing from her aunt. However, she felt it was her duty to go when she received one of her plaintive letters starting,

"This may be the last time that I am able to invite you to

visit me."

Athina had enjoyed the drive.

She had been extremely firm when her chaperone, Mrs. Beckwith, had suggested accompanying her.

"You know long drives give you a headache," she said, "and that Aunt Muriel will treat you as if you are dust beneath her feet. She has never had any time for what she always calls 'superfluous additions to the household' and that I am afraid, is the category that you come into."

They both laughed.

"Well, I know that Gauntlet will look after you," Mrs. Beckwith commented, "and you will be away for only the one night."

"I will be back home in good time for dinner on Tuesday," Athina promised.

She kissed Mrs. Beckwith affectionately and, when she left, she had waved to her as she went down the drive.

Athina's father, the Earl of Murling, had died last year.

He had left his only child a large fortune, a large house and a large estate.

What relatives there were in the vicinity had, immediately after the funeral, asked Athina which of them she intended to reside with.

Alternatively whom she would wish to come to live with her as her chaperone.

"When I looked at their faces," Athina related to Mrs. Beckwith, "I knew that what they were really thinking was how much money Papa had left me and that it must be kept in the family."

"That was actually very sensible of them," Mrs. Beckwith replied.

"Not at all," Athina retorted. "It was just sheer greed. They were afraid that I would be pursued by endless fortune-hunters who would somehow contrive to get their hands on money that might otherwise have been theirs."

"Now you are being cynical," Mrs. Beckwith demurred. "You are too young, dearest, and far too beautiful to look at the world through anything except for rose-coloured glasses."

During that time she taught Athina as if she was a Governess and he lessons had proved an enormous success.

Mrs. Beckwith was an extraordinarily clever Teacher and Athina enjoyed travelling with her in thought and imagination as she hoped one day to travel in reality.

Athina's father had died just before she was eighteen and she was now a very well-educated and intelligent young woman.

The Earl had arranged for her to be presented at Court to Queen Victoria and to have her first Season in London.

But, as she was plunged immediately into deep mourning, it was obviously impossible that summer.

This year, however, the family had agitated her and arranged that she should go to London at the beginning of May.

This was now just about two weeks ahead and Athina was already wondering if she really wished to leave the beautiful countryside.

"I love being here when there are primroses in the hedgerows and daffodils in the Park," she told Mrs. Beckwith. "I cannot believe that anything in London could be any more entrancing."

"You know just as well as I do," Mrs. Beckwith replied, "that you have to meet charming young gentlemen, dance every night at a ball and fulfil your dear father's dream that you will be the 'Belle of the Season'."

Athina laughed.

"Papa wanted me to be that because it would be a compliment to him. He always behaved as if he had created me."

"Which, of course, he indeed had!" Mrs. Beckwith smiled. "If he was here now, I would certainly congratulate him!"

Athina laughed again.

"I have the uncomfortable feeling that both you and my Papa are going to be disappointed. What will happen is that the young men I meet will think I am a 'blue stocking' and avoid me like the plague!"

Mrs. Beckwith put her head on one side and contemplated her pupil.

"I have actually wondered about it myself," she confessed. "You must, Athina, be intelligent enough to let the man always know best, especially when he is wrong."

Athina threw up her hands.

"I refuse! I absolutely refuse! If they will say something stupid, as some of Papa's friends used to do, I shall just find it impossible not to correct them."

"In which case you will have to come back home and talk to the primroses and the daffodils," Mrs. Beckwith warned her.

"And, of course, you, dearest Becky," Athina then added. "I love talking to you and that reminds me that the new book on the Universe has just arrived and we must both read it tonight."

The library at Murling Park was already packed with new books and Athina was far more interested in them than in the clothes that she had been buying to take to London with her.

She had wanted to rent a house in Mayfair and stay there on her own with Mrs. Beckwith.

But there was such an outcry from her relations at the idea that she agreed instead to stay with one of her more amenable aunts.

This particular aunt of hers was married to one of the Gentlemen-in-Waiting at Buckingham Palace and so she had the right *entrée* to all the important functions there.

Mrs. Beckwith had agreed that she would stay in the country at Murling Park and Athina knew that she would miss her dreadfully.

She was still feeling rather dubious as to what she would find in the Social world.

How could it compare with the joy of owning the finest stables in the country?

There were her father's finest horses still stabled at Newmarket and it had been impossible while she was in mourning to attend Race Meetings or indeed any public gathering or any sort.

Queen Victoria had set the fashion for long-drawn-out and over-emphasised black mourning after she lost had her most beloved Prince Albert in 1861.

Athina had therefore been confined to Murling Park and it had not troubled her in the slightest.

She missed her father so much, it would have been impossible for her not to do so.

But Mrs. Beckwith was an amusing and delightful companion.

The many horses, Athina often thought to herself, compensated for having no young men to talk to.

She looked so lovely as she rode off on some spirited stallion that she quickly had under her control that Mrs. Beckwith would watch her and sigh.

Athina was exquisite with her golden curls that had a touch of red in them.

Her grey eyes were unusual.

In fact she had a unique beauty that made her different from all other girls of her age.

It was, Mrs. Beckwith knew well, the reason why she had been Christened Athina after the Greek Goddess.

From the moment she was born she acquired a loveliness that few other babies had.

'I wonder what will happen to her?' Mrs. Beckwith asked herself as Athina trotted off down the drive, her sylph-like figure silhouetted against the darkness of the trees.

The way she rode reminded her of Diana the Huntress.

Now Athina drove her horses into a large courtyard of the Posting inn where there were several carriages of different styles parked at one end.

This meant that the horses had already been taken into the stables and their owners had gone into the inn.

"Don't forget that I am 'Mrs. Beckwith'," Athina warned Gauntlet as she drew the horses to a standstill. Gauntlet then opened the door of the chaise.

Athina stepped out and, as an ostler came hurrying towards them, she said,

"We have urgent need of a blacksmith as we have had an accident to a wheel. I hope that there is one available here or nearby."

"That 'e was just a few minutes ago," the ostler replied.

"Please fetch him quickly for me," Athina urged him.

The ostler hurried off and she turned and smiled at Gauntlet. Then she walked towards the entrance of the inn.

Inside the proprietor was standing inside the low-ceilinged hall and, having appraised the newcomer, he bowed politely to Athina.

"Can I be of help to you, ma'am," he asked.

"I have had an accident to a wheel of my chaise," Athina replied.

The proprietor looked at her quizzically as she went on.

"And so I am hoping that your blacksmith can mend it, but as it is now getting late I must stay the night"

"I'll be able to accommodate you, ma'am," the proprietor nodded.

"I would like your best bedroom," Athina said. "My luggage is at the back of the chaise and I also require a room for my groom."

"That'll be seen to immediately," the proprietor promised her.

He sent a porter scurrying to collect Athina's luggage and then an elderly housemaid in a mob cap was called to show her upstairs.

The stairs were of oak and uncarpeted but well-polished.

The bedroom Athina was shown into was comfortable although, of course, not luxurious. It was on the first floor, which indicated to her that there was nothing better in the inn.

She told the maid that it would suit her and she would be staying for only one night.

"Are you busy at the moment?" Athina asked conversationally as they waited for the porter to bring up the luggage.

"We've a number of gentlemen stayin' on their way 'ome from the Races, ma'am," the maid replied, 'but otherwise things be a bit dull around 'ere."

The porter brought in Athina's small trunk, which was all she had required for the one night stay with her aunt.

As the maid started to unpack for her, she took off her hat, which was somewhat dusty and changed her gown.

By the time she had washed and then brushed her hair, it was dark outside.

She knew, as there was no moon tonight, that it would have been impossible to drive home through the narrow lanes.

'I am far safer here,' she told herself, 'for we might have had a more serious accident if we had continued on that terrible road.'

At the same time she knew that Mrs. Beckwith was expecting her and she would be worried when she did not arrive as she had said she would.

'We will leave directly after breakfast,' she decided, 'and I will be home well before luncheon.'

She told the maid to call her at eight o'clock prompt, thanked her for helping her with her gown and then went downstairs.

The dining room was large and boasted a beamed ceiling like the hall and there was a large fire crackling in the grate.

It had been a cold spring and, although the days were beginning to be turn warmer, it was still chilly at night.

The proprietor was at the foot of the stairs as Athina descended and he waited for her.

"I've kept a table for you, ma'am," he said, "'tis close to the fire and I hopes you'll enjoy your dinner."

"I am sure I shall," Athina answered him.

She had remembered when the housemaid was not looking to slip a ring onto the third finger of her left hand. It was a pretty ring with three diamonds and had belonged to her mother.

By twisting it ground so that the diamonds were on the inside of her hand, it looked like a Wedding ring.

The proprietor escorted her to the table that he had described and Athina was pleased to find that she was on her own in the dining room.

The rest of the tables were occupied at the other end of the room.

When she had ordered all that she wanted to eat, the proprietor hurried away to the kitchen.

She was then able to look round at her fellow guests.

At one table there were three elegantly dressed young men. They were laughing and joking with each other too loudly while apparently celebrating or anticipating a win at the Races.

At two of the other tables there were what Athina thought must be commercial travellers.

Then there was an elderly couple. The woman had a red shawl over her shoulders and she guessed that they were staying in the inn and were not just travellers.

She then started in her mind to make up stories about each of the guests as she often did when she saw strangers in the countryside and villages.

Then at the other side of the fireplace she saw that there was a man who was obviously a gentleman. And with him was a small boy.

She had not noticed them at first, but she was made aware of their presence when she could overhear the gentleman speaking sharply to the waiter.

He had apparently brought him a bottle of wine that was different from the one that he had ordered and the gentleman cursed the waiter for being stupid.

Looking at the gentleman without appearing to do so, she thought that he looked disagreeable and clearly bad-tempered. She suspected that he was also a heavy drinker.

The little boy with him was obviously very young and she made a guess that he was about nine years of age.

He had fair hair and seemed a rather delicate child and Athina thought that he also looked very tired.

She wondered where they were going and what their relationship was.

Her dinner arrived after only a short wait and she started to eat.

As she did so, she heard the gentleman start complaining about the food and sending away one dish because in his view the meat was cut too thickly.

She ruminated that, whoever he might be, her father would have disapproved of him.

"I dislike men who shout at waiters," he had said to her once.

He himself had never shouted at his servants. If he rebuked them, it was in a cool quiet manner that was far more effective than if he had raged at them.

The gentleman, who obviously had ordered a large meal, was still complaining as Athina finished hers.

She felt that, while the food admittedly was not very exciting, it was edible and on the whole well cooked.

She had also been attended to without there being any long waits.

When she thanked the waiter for his excellent service, he said,

"It's bin a pleasure waitin' on you, ma'am."

She smiled and left the dining room.

She could still hear the gentleman's voice blasting away by the time she had reached the foot of the stairs.

A porter hurried to stop her before she went any further.

"Your groom, ma'am," he said, "'as told me to tell you that the wheels of your chaise 'as now bin repaired."

"Thank you," Athina replied.

Once in her bedroom she undressed and then found that she was unexpectedly tired.

Listening to her aunt saying the same things over and over again that she had heard so often before was always exhausting.

They had also come quite a long distance to where they were now.

'I should sleep well,' Athina told herself.

She said her prayers and as she said them she felt, as she always did, that her father was close to her.

Also her beloved mother, whom she had adored and who had died two years previously.

They had both been, she recalled, charming and delightful people.

The sad thing was that they did not get on and did not even like each other.

Indeed it had taken Athina some years before she had realised just how divided her parents really were.

It was all due to the fact that theirs, as with most aristocrats, had been an arranged marriage.

When she was old enough to talk to her mother intelligently, the Countess had confided in her.

When she was young she had fallen very much in love with the son of the neighbouring Squire.

"We had known each other since we were children," the Countess said. "Then, when I was seventeen and he was twenty-one, we realised that we were in love."

"How romantic, Mama!" Athina had exclaimed. "What did you do about it?"

"We used to meet secretly," the Countess said, "as William did not wish to approach my father until he had completed his degree at Oxford University and had seen a little of the world."

"So he went abroad, Mama?"

"Only for a short time. When he came back we knew that we were more in love with each other than we had been before. William then decided that he would talk to my father."

There was a note in the Countess's voice as she spoke that made Athina ask,

"What happened then?"

"It had all been arranged that I should go to London that spring to be presented at Court and to have a Season in which I was to enjoy the balls. William then asked me if I wanted to wait until after I had been presented before he asked Papa if we could be engaged. I stupidly said that perhaps I should be presented first."

She sighed before she went on,

"I thought that it would make me seem more grown-up and more capable of knowing my own mind."

"Then you did suspect that your father would not really welcome William as a son-in-law," Athina had suggested.

"I was sure that my father would want me to make an important marriage."

"Because you were so beautiful," Athina had finished.

Her mother smiled.

"I think that was the reason and also my father was an ambitious man who had somehow failed to become of any significance himself in the neibourhood."

"So what happened?" Athina had asked.

"Foolishly I went to London. I was then presented at Buckingham Palace and, while I was there, your father saw me – "

Now there was a note in her mother's voice that Athina could not help recognising was one of despair.

"And Papa fell in love with you," she murmured.

"He wanted to marry me," her mother replied, "mainly because he needed a young wife who would give him the son he wanted."

Athina just stared at her mother thinking that this was something that she had never realised before.

"He talked to my father and mother," the Countess went on, "and, of course, they were completely overjoyed that I should marry anyone as prestigious as the Earl of Murling. They had never aspired so high even though I was thought to be very pretty."

"And what happened to William?" Athina had asked.

Her mother made a helpless gesture.

"I was forced to say 'goodbye' to him and it broke his heart as it broke mine."

"Was there nothing you could do to persuade your father that you loved him?"

"I tried to tell him," the Countess said, "but he would not listen to me. Everybody thought that I was the luckiest girl in the world to have captured an Earl before I was even launched onto the Social world! So we were married."

Her mother did not say anything more.

Athina, however, knew that she had never loved the man who she had been forced to marry.

What is more he had been seriously disappointed in her.

It might have been Fate, or it might have simply been because she was unhappy, that the Countess had produced only one child and that was a daughter.

The doctors had said that they thought it was impossible for her to bear any more children.

At first the Earl would not listen to them, saying that he had never heard such nonsense. His wife was young and beautiful and so it was only a question of time.

But the longed-for son did not arrive.

He was therefore forced to accept the fact that Athina would be his only child. So he was determined to make her exceptional.

It was his way of hiding the truth that he was bitterly disappointed that the son he wanted so desperately would never materialise.

Loving both her parents, Athina found it very hard not to be aware every day and every hour how much they resented each other.

She would often talk animatedly and excitedly to her father on a number of different subjects

But, when her mother came into the room, it seemed suddenly as if the temperature had dropped. There was a restriction over whatever they said that she could not ignore.

Then Athina's mother had died in one very cold winter when she contracted pneumonia.

It had passed through Athina's mind that maybe her father would marry again, but he was very obviously too old.

Over sixty years old, he had made the best of his life by making his daughter his companion instead of the son he craved for.

He therefore carried on, Athina thought with some relief without a wife who he had always felt frustrated with.

When he had taken a nasty fall when out hunting, the doctors had claimed that it was nothing serious.

But he died a week later.

It seemed unbelievable to Athina that she should then suddenly find herself all alone.

The one thing she had learnt from her parents' marriage was that never in any circumstances would she marry a man who she did not love.

'Never, never,' she told herself, 'will I live like Papa and Mama – both so very charming in themselves and still both so unhappy as apart from me they had nothing in common."

She was not certain what sort of man she really wanted to have in her life.

But one thing in her life she did realise – she would never allow anybody, whoever they might be, to choose her husband for her.

Almost as soon as the funeral was over, that was exactly what her relations had wanted to do.

They swept into the house, one after another and the conversation was always the same.

"You cannot live alone, Athina dear, and the sooner we find you a suitable husband the better!"

"I have no wish to be married," Athina always answered firmly.

"That is quite ridiculous," would be the answer. "You are already eighteen and, if you are not careful, you will be on the shelf and an old maid."

They would laugh at the idea, but Athina knew that it was what they believed was the truth.

"You will meet plenty of gentlemen in London," one relative after another had insisted.

Even before she had finished her last months of mourning, they began to bring men into the house to meet her.

"Lord Newcomb is staying with us for two days," an aunt would say, "and it seems a pity, as he is here in the country, for you not to meet him."

Or else the plan might be,

"I know that Sir Willoughby would be thrilled to see your father's horses. Take him round the stables, Athina dear, while I sit in front of the fire."

As soon as they arrived, Athina felt that every nerve of hers was on edge.

Her whole self rebelled at the thought that the newcomer was just there for one reason only.

To look her over as if she was on show at a fashionable Spring Horse Fair.

'No! No! *No!*' she wanted to scream out. 'Go away and leave me alone. I don't want to marry you or anybody else.'

However, one of the many things her father had taught her was self-control.

She was always charming and polite and no one had the slightest idea of what she was really feeling inside.

One man, more importunate than the rest, returned unexpectedly and alone the next day.

When he had actually proposed to her, she replied with what was in her mind,

"I am, of course, honoured, my Lord," she said in a cold voice, that after such a very short acquaintance you should ask me to be your wife, but I must make it very clear that I have no intention of marrying anyone."

"That is ridiculous!" he had replied. "Of course you will have to be married. No woman should live alone and certainly no one quite as beautiful as you."

"I have plenty of people to look after me and, although you may think it rather strange, I like being alone with, of course, my horses, my friends and my estate."

She saw a look in his eyes, which told her that her estate was as desirable to him as she was herself. In fact without it it was doubtful if he would have been so eager.

She held out her hand.

"Goodbye, my Lord, and I thank you for calling, but I think that you will understand when I tell you that it would be a mistake for you to come here again."

There was nothing that her ardent suitor could do but leave and she told herself with a little smile that it was with his tail between his legs.

Athina stretched herself out on the goose feather mattress, which was very comfortable and closed her eyes.

Tomorrow, she thought, she would be home and that was where she wanted to be.

It was then, as she was just about falling asleep, that she heard a scream.

CHAPTER TWO

It was the high scream of something small that was frightened.

As Athina listened, she heard a harsh voice say,

"I have been waiting for you! Where the devil have you been?"

It was easy to recognise the voice of the gentleman who had dined opposite her and who had been so offensive to the waiters.

He was speaking to the little boy who had been with him and she heard the boy stammering his reply,

"I – went to – the stables. I thought – Ladybird was – unhappy because you – had whipped her."

"It has nothing to do with you whether I whip my horses or not," the gentleman said angrily, "and you will not go out of the inn unless I tell you to. It is time you learnt how to behave yourself."

He must have made a threatening gesture for the boy cried out.

"Please – I am – sorry. Don't – beat me – again!"

"I am going to teach you to obey me!" the gentleman thundered.

There was another scream and Athina thought that the child must be trying to escape.

There was a noise as if two people were scuffling.

Then there was a thud as if the boy had been thrown onto the bed.

He was screaming again, screaming so that if was unbearable to hear him.

With hands that trembled Athina relit the candle that she had just blown out.

When there was a light in the room, she realised exactly why she was hearing what was happening so clearly.

It was because there was a communicating door between her and the boy's bedroom and she had not noticed it before.

The screams were gradually growing weaker and now the child was mumbling and she thought that he was mumbling,

"Mum-ma! *Mum-ma*!"

"That will teach you not to disobey me again," the gentleman said in the same aggressive voice. "I will beat obedience into you if it is the last thing I do."

Athina heard him walk across the room and open the door to slam it shut behind him. She also thought that she heard him turn the key in the lock.

She climbed out of bed and, putting on her dressing gown, went to the communicating door.

Now the boy was just sobbing away piteously as if he had not the strength to make any loud sound.

Athina knew that she had to help him.

She looked at the door and saw that there was a key on her side of it. She turned it in the lock and then opened the door cautiously.

She did this just in case she had been mistaken and the gentleman was still there in the boy's room.

By the light of two candles she could see that the room was much smaller than hers and there was just a single bed on which the boy was lying face down.

His coat must have been pulled off him because it was lying in a heap on the floor and he was wearing only his shirt and trousers.

She went into the room.

As she drew nearer to him, she could see blood from the weals on his back beginning to stain the whiteness of his shirt.

He was sobbing convulsively, while at the same time murmuring, 'Mum-ma! *Mum-ma*!' in a broken little voice.

She sat down on the bed and put her hand very gently on his fair head,

"It's all right," she said in a soft voice. "It's all over now and he will not hurt you anymore."

For a moment the boy was still.

Then he raised himself up on his arms as if to look at her, but his eyes were swollen and blinded by his tears.

"It's all right now," Athina said again. "I will not let him hurt you anymore."

It was then that the small boy flung himself against her.

He clung onto her, saying, 'Mum-ma! *Mum-ma!*' as if he thought that she really was his mother.

She wanted to take him in her arms, but was afraid of hurting his back. Instead she held him by his shoulders and then continued to say quietly,

"It's all right. It's all over."

It was some time before his tears ceased.

When they did stop, Athina suggested,

"Now come into my room and I will put something on your back that will take away the pain."

The boy held onto her for a moment as if he was afraid that she was going to leave him.

Then, as she rose slowly to her feet, she helped him to the ground.

His small face was wet with tears and she had to guide him round the bed and out of the room into hers.

Only when she had closed the door behind her and locked it did she say in a normal tone of voice,

"No one can hear us now and I am going to make you feel very much better than you do at the moment."

She made him sit down on her bed.

Going over to the washstand she then brought back a sponge and a linen towel.

Gently she washed his face, holding the sponge against his eyes to cool them. He sat still as she did so and while she dried his face with a white towel.

Now that she could see him clearly she realised that he was a very god-looking little boy.

There was no doubt that he was suffering from shock and was, she thought, not quite certain about what was happening.

"I am going to put some cream on your back," she said quietly, "so take off your shirt."

He fumbled with the buttons and in the end she had to help him.

When she then took the shirt away from him, she gave a gasp of horror.

His whole back was covered with weals from the whip that the gentleman had used so brutally on him and she could see that there were many other weals from previous whippings.

She thought that it would be a mistake to try to make him give her an explanation.

She next went over to the dressing table and came back with the cream that she used on her face when her skin was dry from the winter winds.

She always used it when she had been out hunting or when, like today, she had been covered with dust.

She turned the small boy round a little so that she could sit behind him.

"I will try not to hurt you," she said, "but this cream of mine will soon start healing your skin. In the meantime it will prevent the weals from hurting you quite so much."

She applied it carefully as she was more horrified every moment as she realised how often the child had been beaten.

Then, without telling him what she was doing, she went back to his room next door to fetch his nightshirt. She had noticed it lying at the end of the bed.

She slipped it over his head.

And then she told him,

"You will be much more comfortable now and if you go to sleep you will feel much better in the morning."

As she spoke, she realised that the little boy was looking at her as if he was seeing her for the first time.

"I want my Mum-ma," he insisted, "but she has gone away and – will never come – back."

She could hardly hear what he said and the pain in his voice and in his eyes was unmistakable.

"Your mother is dead?" Athina asked him.

The boy nodded.

He was looking at her like a small animal who did not understand what was happening to him.

She knew that he was thinking that he did not want to leave her.

"I will tell you what we will do," she suggested. "If you take off your trousers, you can get into bed and tell me about your mother."

As if it was an order, he rose gingerly to his feet and slipped off his trousers beneath his nightshirt.

Rather carefully because his back was obviously hurting him, he climbed into the bed.

It was a large one and there was plenty of room for Athina to get in on the other side.

She then put her head down on the pillow and, as if he knew that she expected him to do the same, he lay down facing her.

"Now," she said, "we can talk without being overheard. First you must tell me what your name is."

"It is Peter – Peter Naver."

"And who is the man who is being so unkind to you?"

There was a little pause before Peter answered,

"He is – my stepfather. Mum-ma married him – after Papa was – killed."

"And you live with him?" Athina enquired.

"Yes – he is my – Guardian."

Athina knew only too well that Guardians had complete control over their Wards.

At the same time it seemed strange to her that a stepfather should want to keep the child of his dead wife.

"Have you no other relations?" she queried.

"We have been to see – my grandmother today," Peter answered, "and she – asked me to – stay with her, but Step-Papa would – not let me."

"Why not?" Athina asked.

Peter made a helpless gesture with his hands and she was aware that he had no answer to that question.

"What was your mother's name before she married your Papa?" she then tried.

Peter could answer this.

"She was – Lady Louise Rock and – I miss her so much. I wish I – could die and be – with her."

He was crying again and instinctively Athina reached out to draw him nearer to her.

He put his head against her shoulder.

"I want my Mum-ma," he repeated. "I want – to be – with her."

"I know you do," Athina said, "but she is near you even though you cannot see her and she is naturally very upset to think that you are so unhappy."

Peter stopped crying.

"She is near me? Really – near to me?" he then asked. "Like the – angels?"

"Yes, just like that," Athina smiled, "and I expect your mother once told you that you had a Guardian Angel watching over you and now she is looking after you too."

"Are you – sure? Quite – sure?" Peter wanted to know.

"Of course I am," Athina replied.

"Then why does – she let – Step-Papa be so – cruel to me? He – beats me and beats me – nothing I – do is right."

"It is something we must prevent happening ever again," Athina asserted.

She thought that Peter was thinking over what she had said and went on,

"I do want to help you, Peter, and I think it was your mother who brought me here tonight so that I could learn exactly how cruelly your stepfather is treating you and take you away from him."

As she spoke, it was as if someone else was putting the words into her mouth and it struck her that, although it was a strange thing to say, she had to say it.

"So you really will – take me – away from – Step-Papa?" Peter asked eagerly.

"I will certainly do my best," Athina answered, "but you will have to tell me a little more about your mother. You say her name was Lady Louise Rock?"

"Yes – that is – right," Peter confirmed. "She lived in a big house, which was – also called 'Rock' and I always thought it was a – funny name for a – house."

Athina gave an exclamation.

"Are you telling me," she next asked, "that your mother was the daughter of the Marquis of Rockingdale?"

Peter nodded.

"She used to – tell me about – my grandfather who was a – very important man. His house, which is called 'Rock Park', is very – very big."

Athina found this hard to believe.

She knew Rock Park, of course, she did. It was very near where she herself lived.

She had never been to the house although her parents had been invited to parties there over the years.

The Marquis of Rockingdale had died two or three years ago and her father had said that he had no use for the son who had succeeded to the title of Marquis.

"He spends all his time in London," he said to Athina, "with a lot of beautiful women instead of attending to his estate. I have no time for those young toffs who think they are the 'Smart Set'."

Athina had, however, hoped that, when she too was grown up, she would be invited to visit Rock Park.

She wanted to see the inside of the house. Her father and mother had described it to her in detail and it was actually one of the sights of the County.

The estate was extremely large and at one point bordered with her father's. She had hunted over some of it a few years ago, but that was only by accident as she had become lost.

The last Marquis, because he had grown so old, did not ride to hounds.

The present one preferred to hunt in Leicestershire, where he had a smart Hunting Lodge.

Nevertheless what was important at the moment was that he was the uncle of this wretched defenceless little boy and he would have to do something about the way he was being treated.

"When did your mother leave you?" she asked him gently.

"A long time ago," Peter replied, "when I was just six and now I am nearly – ten."

'Almost four years of this appalling devil torturing the poor boy,' Athina thought to herself.

It seemed very strange that none of the family knew about what was happening.

Peter was still cuddling against her and she quizzed him,

"Why then did you not tell your grandmama when she asked you to stay with her that you were unhappy with your stepfather?"

"I wanted to," Peter said, "but Step-Papa was in the room and he – gripped my arm and – said, 'Peter wants to stay with me, do you not, Peter?'"

Peter drew in his breath.

"I could – not say 'no' as he was – pinching my arm – pinching it so – hard that it – hurt me."

Athina thought that the more she heard about Peter's stepfather, the more she loathed him.

Now she asked Peter somewhat belatedly,

"You have not told me your stepfather's name."

"He is – Lord B-Burnham of A-Avon," Peter said, faltering a little over the words. "He is very – important in the House of Lords and – everybody is – frightened of him."

There was silence for a moment.

And then he went on as if he was talking to himself,

"I am – frightened and his – horses are – frightened. Ladybird is – unhappy tonight, I know – she is – unhappy."

"Which is why you went off to see her," Athina suggested softly. "That was very brave and kind of you."

"I love Ladybird and I love – all Step-Papa's – horses and when he – whips them I – know what – they are feeling."

He made a little movement as he spoke as if his back was really hurting him.

Athina knew now that she had heard quite enough and she was absolutely determined that Lord Burnham would no longer be able to terrorise and torture his stepson.

Very gently she turned and put Peter's head down on the pillow beside her.

"Now you go to sleep, Peter. In the morning we are going to do something very exciting and I don't want you to be tired."

"I am tired now," Peter said. "It was a – long drive. We went a – very long – way and the – dust made my throat – dry, but – Step-Papa would – not let me – have any – water."

Athina felt that, if she heard any more about Lord Burnham, she would murder him with her own hands.

She knew instinctively that she would have to be clever if she was to save poor little Peter from his ghastly stepfather.

She kissed his cheek and he put his arms round her neck.

"You are like Mum-ma," he whispered, "just like my Mum-ma."

"Then go to sleep and dream about her," Athina answered, "and remember that she is here beside you looking after you and she has told me to help you escape."

"From – Step-Papa?"

"From your Step-Papa," Athina confirmed to him.

It was a vow rather than a promise.

After all the small boy had been through, he was so exhausted that he fell asleep almost immediately.

Athina leant over him and blew out the candle and then she lay planning what she should do.

She realised that it would be difficult to spirit Peter away from the inn without having a scene with Lord Burnham.

She therefore willed herself to wake up at five o'clock when she knew that the maids would be stirring.

Her father had been in the Army and he had taught her how to wake up, as he could, at whatever hour she pleased.

"It is just a question of willpower," he had told her, "and telling your subconscious to carry out your wishes so that there is no need for a reveille or alarms of any sort."

Athina at the age of twelve had found this a tough challenge and soon she could wake, as her father could, at any time she desired.

But now she forced herself to relax.

She was already planning in her mind how she would take Peter away from the inn without Lord Burnham being aware of it.

She also said a very special prayer not only to God but to Lady Louise as well that she would be successful with her plan.

'I have to save your little son from that brute,' she said to her in her prayer, '"but you will have to help me. It may not be easy, but I am quite sure when your brother knows what is happening he will take correct action.'

She only hoped that she was right.

As if Lady Louise had answered her prayer, she then fell asleep.

Neither she nor Peter moved an inch until it was five o'clock in the morning.

*

Athina awoke and for a moment she could not remember where she was.

Then she could see the small fair head on the pillow next to hers and recalled what had happened last night.

She climbed out of bed very quietly so as not to disturb Peter and opened the door onto the corridor.

As she had expected, she could hear movements down below the stairs. The maids were already at work cleaning the entrance hall and the dining room.

She waited until one of them passed by at the bottom of the stairs and then, raising her voice, she called out,

"Good morning."

The maid looked up and saw her.

"I am Mrs. Beckwith," Athina said. "Would you be so kind as to tell my groom that I wish to have my chaise round at the front door in half an hour?"

"I'll tell 'im, ma'am," the maid replied, bobbing a little curtsey.

Athina went back into her room and started to dress and she then packed her trunk.

Going into Peter's room, she collected his coat, which was still on the floor. She saw too that he had a leather bag in which all his other things were packed.

She guessed that Lord Burnham would have brought a valet with him, who also attended to Peter.

She knew that this could be dangerous as the man would certainly be up earlier than his Master.

She went back into her own room and locked the communicating door between their two rooms.

Then she woke up Peter, who sat up rubbing his eyes.

"I was – dreaming," he said, "dreaming that Mumma was back – with me."

Athina kissed him and said,

"She *was* with you. Now listen to me, Peter, if we are to escape, you will have to dress quickly and then I will tell you what to do."

"Can I really go – away with – you?" Peter asked hesitantly.

"That is what you are going to do," Athina answered, "but hurry!"

He jumped out of bed at once and started to put on his clothes.

He did it so quickly that Athina recognised that he was well used to dressing himself. And all that she had to do was to tie the laces of his shoes.

By this time it was after half past five.

She knew that if Gauntlet had received her message, he would be already in the courtyard.

The vital issue was that Peter should go through the hall and into the yard without being questioned.

"Now listen to me, Peter, I want you to go downstairs just as you did last night when you went out to see Ladybird."

"Am I to – see her – now?"

"No, you must not," Athina said, "as your stepfather's groom or his valet might see you."

Peter seemed to understand and she went on,

"Go out through the side door into the yard and, when you get there, hurry as quickly as you can towards the gate."

"The gate we – came in by?"

"Yes, that is the one I mean. Then turn right – do you know which is right?"

Peter held out his right hand to prove that he did.

"Good. Then go right and walk along the road but don't run. Just walk and I will join you in the chaise as quickly as I can."

"Then I – will get – in the chaise with – you?" Peter asked rather pathetically.

"That is the idea," Athina answered. "Don't talk to anybody. Just do exactly as I have told you. It is absolutely imperative that nobody should notice you."

"No one – noticed me – last night," Peter pointed out.

"But then it was dark," Athina reminded him, "and, although it is very early in the morning, people may be moving about."

Peter nodded his head as if he fully understood what Athina was saying to him.

She smiled at him.

"Off you go then and just walk casually along the road."

She let him out through the door and she waited until she felt that he would by now be outside the inn before she went downstairs.

A porter in his shirtsleeves was clearing away empty beer mugs.

"Would you please be so kind as to bring down the two pieces of luggage that are upstairs in my bedroom?" Athina asked him.

He looked up in surprise because she was about so early.

At the same time, because she spoke with a tone of authority, he replied, 'yes, ma'am,' and then ran up the stairs immediately.

Athina went to the reception desk and was glad to see that there was no sign of the proprietor.

There was, however, a porter who appeared to be in charge.

She asked him what she owed and paid the bill, leaving a good tip for the staff.

He thanked her and she then hurried through the door and into the yard.

With some sense of relief she saw Gauntlet waiting for her with the horses between the shafts.

"Good morning, Gauntlet," she said. "I was afraid you might not have received my message."

"'Mornin', ma'am. I were a bit surprised at your ladyship wantin' to leave so early," Gauntlet replied.

Athina did not answer.

She was busy getting into the riding seat and picking up the reins.

As she did so, the porter who had gone to fetch her luggage came out of the inn.

He was carrying her small trunk and Peter's leather bag.

Quickly, before Gauntlet could question the strange leather bag, she said to him,

"That is my bag too. Put them both in please."

Gauntlet did as he was told at once and Athina handed him a half-sovereign to give to the porter.

It was a large tip, but she hoped that, if there was any commotion over the disappearance of Peter, he would not want to involve her.

As soon as Gauntlet was beside her, she drove off.

She turned the horses to the right as they left the entrance to the courtyard.

As she did so, she looked down the road, but could see no sign of Peter.

For a moment she felt her heart stop.

What could have happened to him?

Had he been apprehended by his Lordship's valet?

Or had he misunderstood her simple instructions?

Then, as the horses moved further on, she saw him coming out of a hedgerow where he must have been hiding.

She gave a sigh of relief.

It told her more forcefully than any words could how much the small boy already meant to her.

She had known last night that she would do anything – anything to save him from the bestial cruelty of Lord Burnham.

Although it seemed to her just too incredible, she was quite sure that she was being directed.

And guided by a Power that was not of this world.

To Gauntlet sitting beside her she said,

"We are not going straight home, but to Rock Park."

Gauntlet did not seem very surprised.

He only replied,

"There be two grooms at the inn who'd been at the Races. They'd made a bet on 'is Lordship's 'orse."

Athina thought that they must have been in the employment of the young man in the dining room.

They also had doubtless backed the winner.

As she drove on, Gauntlet said as if he was speaking to himself,

"'Is Lordship'll be the next Master of the Horse now that Lord Edward Rock be dead."

Athina had read of Lord Edward's death in *The Times* and she had not been particularly interested although her father had known him.

Now she said,

"You see that small boy just ahead. He is coming with us to Rock Park."

She thought that Gauntlet would ask her all sorts of questions. But he merely nodded and replied,

"Very good, my Lady, and Rock Park be on our way 'ome."

"I know," Athina answered him.

She pulled the horses to a standstill beside Peter and he climbed into the chaise.

"We have – done it! *We have done – it*!" he cried excitedly.

Without saying anything more, Gauntlet moved into a seat behind and Peter sat beside Athina.

He moved close to her and put his cheek on her arm.

"I was – so frightened," he said, "in case – you did not – come or Step-Papa had been able to – stop you."

"Did you see anybody you recognised as you walked through the courtyard?" Athina asked.

Peter shook his head.

"I hurried, as you told me, and there was nobody about except the man who was with these horses."

"That is Gauntlet and he is my groom," Athina explained. "It was clever of you to get away without being seen."

"Step-Papa will be very – very – angry when he – finds me gone," Peter murmured.

"I know," Athina nodded.

"He – will – beat me again."

"He will have to find you first," Athina replied, "and I will tell you where we are going. We are going to Rock Park to see your uncle who, as I expect you know, is the Marquis of Rockingdale."

"Will he – stop Step-Papa from – beating me?" Peter asked.

"I know he will," Athina answered.

As she spoke, she thought that whatever the Marquis was like, he could not allow the child to be so appallingly treated.

'Lord Burnham is a beast!' she told herself. 'If the Marquis has any guts, as my father would say, he will tell him so.'

Peter made himself comfortable.

At the same time he was still sitting very close to her.

It was as if he felt that she protected him and there was no chance of his being snatched away unexpectedly.

Because Athina could feel his fear vibrating from him, she drove faster than she would have done otherwise.

Once again they had to turn off into the narrow lane where they had clashed with the farm wagon the previous night.

She was careful, but she was now in a greater hurry than she had been the night before.

Every minute that passed brought them nearer to the time when Peter's absence at the inn would be discovered.

Lord Burnham would either send his valet or would go himself to the boy's bedroom and find it empty.

He had locked the door into the corridor and so he would quickly realise that Peter must have left through the communicating door.

To make things even more difficult, Athina had locked that door on her side.

She then put the key in one of the drawers of the dressing table.

At least there would have to be a further delay until the key was found.

She also guessed that Lord Burnham, however determined he was to search for his stepson, would not leave the inn without first having breakfast.

Athina was sure that Lord Burnham was a very astute man.

Therefore, when he was convinced that Peter was not in the inn or the stables, he would know that someone had helped him to escape.

He would soon learn from the servants that she and Gauntlet had left the inn very early in the morning and he would be told as well that she had occupied the adjacent room.

There was therefore every probable likelihood that Peter had gone away with her.

It would certainly seem more likely than that Peter had gone with the racegoers, the commercial travellers or indeed anyone else staying in the inn last night.

It took Athina nearly two hours before she could turn in at the high and impressive wrought-iron gold-tipped gates of Rock Park.

As she went up the drive lined with ancient oak trees, she found herself praying that the Marquis would be in residence.

Also that he would understand the situation and hopefully thank her for taking Peter away from the dreadful man who was treating him so abominably.

'How can he be anything but grateful?' she asked herself several times.

Equally, remembering some of the stories that she had heard of the Marquis's reputation, she was not so sure.

She next looked ahead of her up the gravel drive.

Rock Park was a truly magnificent building.

The sun then came out and it seemed suddenly to illuminate the Marquis's standard on the flagpole above the roof and it waved slowly in the light morning breeze.

The fact that the standard was flying meant that the Marquis was indeed in residence.

Athina's heart gave a leap.

She was sure that it was a good omen.

CHAPTER THREE

The Marquis of Rockingdale drove his dog cart down Piccadilly.

He was not surprised that people stared at him in admiration.

He had just received his new dog cart from his coachbuilders and it was partly of his own design.

The dog cart had become fashionable lately and was modelled on the phaeton, which had been in constant use amongst the bucks and beaux of the Regency.

The wheels were reduced in size and the body itself was not so high.

The new look had delighted many of the Country Squires and this was because their dogs could run underneath it, which protected them from being endangered by other traffic.

The Marquis had trained two highly bred Dalmatians to run under a dog cart that he had already acquired. And with the new one there would be more room for the dogs.

Painted black with yellow wheels and upholstery it was striking in itself.

It was indeed even more striking, however, when it was drawn by Sampson. This was a jet-black stallion that had already won a number of prizes.

What the Marquis did not appreciate was that he himself was even more striking than his conveyance.

He wore a shining black top hat on one side of his dark head and a yellow waistcoat that matched the vehicle.

He undoubtedly attracted the attention of every woman he passed and at the same time every man looked enviously at his horse.

It was a warm and sunny day and the ladies on their way to Rotten Row were riding in open Victorias. And they were holding tiny lace-trimmed sunshades over their elaborate hats.

One after another they waved at the Marquis and he had hardly replaced his hat before he had to raise it again.

He noticed the Countess of Gaythorne, who he had had an ardent *affaire de coeur* with the year before. He retained a certain affection for her although he had left her.

This was because she had been far too demonstrative in public and the one thing that the Marquis disliked was parading his feelings to all and sundry.

It gave the gossips even more to talk about than they had already.

It was not surprising that they talked about him. He was not only extremely handsome, but ne was the owner of an ancient title that was part of English history.

He was also immensely rich.

Apart from this he had an intelligent mind and could on occasions be exceedingly witty.

Men liked him even though they were very jealous not only of his many possessions but also of his achievements.

He was an outstanding rider, a first class polo player and excelled at every sport that he cared to be interested in.

Travelling a little further along the road the Marquis then passed the Countess of Stretton.

She had been acclaimed universally as one of the great beauties of the century. She nodded her head to him, but there was a coolness in the look that she gave him.

This was because he had not yet succumbed to her attractions.

Almost every other gentleman in the Social world was ready to be at her beck and call, but so far, however, the Marquis had eluded her very obvious charms.

There was something fastidious in his make-up, which told him that he did not wish to be one of a queue.

If other gentlemen pursued any particular woman, it was typical of the Marquis to turn in the opposite direction.

The truth was, he told himself, that he wanted something unique in his life.

Then he laughed because it was a very difficult thing to find in the Social Set that he moved in.

In fact, if a woman was beautiful, it was inevitable that the Prince of Wales would be there first and after that there would be a scramble amongst the smart young gentlemen.

They, just like the Marquis, were always looking for someone to amuse them.

The Marquis was at this very moment, however, not thinking of women, but of the interview that he was about to have with the Lord Chamberlain.

He had waited he had thought for quite a considerable time.

And now what he most desired was distinctly within his grasp.

It was traditional for the Head of the Rockingdale Family to be the Monarch's Master of the Horse.

The Earls of Rockingdale had held this unique position under both King George III and King George IV.

It was at the end of George IV's reign that the Earldom was made into a Marquisate.

And the first Marquis of Rockingdale was therefore Master of the Horse to King William IV and the n the young Queen Victoria.

Unfortunately he died in a hunting accident when he was not yet fifty and the present Marquis's father refused the position outright.

He claimed that he had no wish to spend his time at Court with so much bowing and scraping, but he hoped, however, that his son would have different ideas.

But his son was at the time only a small boy and the position was instead given to his uncle, Lord Edward Rock, who did perform his duties reasonably well.

Equally he did not have very many horses himself and was not an outstanding owner as his predecessors had been.

Now that the young Marquis had succeeded his father and Lord Edward Pock having died, he looked forward with pleasure to taking his place as the Master of the Horse.

He had already thought of the many improvements that he would make to the Royal Stables.

He was making a formal call on the Earl of Latham, who was the Lord Chamberlain whose office was in St. James's Palace where he dealt with all the details connected with Court Ceremonial.

The Marquis drove in considerable style down St. James's Street.

He was aware that the members of White's Club who were going in and out of the Club were gazing at him. Some, he knew, must be curious as to where he might be going.

He reached St. James's Palace and drew up his horse outside the main door.

When he stepped down from his dog cart, his place was taken by his groom, who had been sitting behind him with his arms folded in the correct manner. He was wearing the splendid Rockingdale livery and a cockaded top hat.

The Marquis then walked into St. James's Palace and there was no need for anybody to guide him to the Lord Chamberlain's office.

He had been there frequently and the Earl of Latham was a man he both respected and liked.

As he appeared, the Earl rose from the chair where he was sitting and held out his hand.

He was a tall and handsome man, whose hair and beard were just beginning to turn a little white and he cut a most distinguished figure at Queen Victoria's drawing rooms and on every State occasion.

"Good morning, Denzil," he greeted him as the Marquis appeared. "I was expecting you."

"I thought you would be, my Lord," the Marquis replied.

"I hear you had a winner two days ago," the Earl said, "but that is nothing unusual."

The Marquis smiled and sat down in a chair in front of the Lord Chamberlain's desk.

"You know, of course, why I have called to see you," the Marquis said. "I need not tell you that I am impatient to take up the position of the Master of the Horse."

He paused for a moment to clear his throat before he continued,

"I wish to implement the improvements and alterations that I have discussed with you on various occasions."

The Lord Chamberlain did not immediately reply and the Marquis looked at him enquiringly before finally he said slowly,

"I am afraid, Denzil, that I have something to tell you."

The Marquis raised his eyebrows.

"To tell me?" he questioned sharply.

"I know that you are expecting to be appointed the Master of the Horse as your forebears were," the Earl continued.

"That is just why I am here," the Marquis answered. "But are you telling me that Her Majesty wishes to appoint someone else?"

There was a note in his voice as if he assumed that the Earl would immediately 'poo-poo' such a suggestion.

Instead he said in a somewhat embarrassed manner,

"It is not quite as bad as that."

"Then what can it be?" the Marquis asked. "Surely Her Majesty is aware that, while it was wrong of my father to refuse the office when it was offered to him, I think it is something he later much regretted."

He sighed before he carried on,

"He was, as you will know, not well at the time, having injured his back in a fall out hunting. He felt the responsibility would be too much for him. So it passed to his brother who was not what you would call an outstanding horseman."

"I am aware of that," the Lord Chamberlain replied, "and Her Majesty appreciates that you have every right to feel that the position should be yours. She will in fact confirm the appointment to you. But on one condition."

"Condition?" the Marquis exclaimed. "So what can you possibly mean by that?"

Again the Lord Chamberlain paused.

He was very fond of the Marquis, whom he had known since he was a small boy and, because he was a kindly man, he was finding this a particularly unpleasant interview.

There was again a silence before the Lord Chamberlain said,

"Her Majesty is willing to appoint you as Master of the Horse, but she considers it most important that you should first be married or at least engaged."

As he finished, the Marquis stared at the Lord Chamberlain as if he felt that what he had heard could not be in any way true.

"*Married?*" he queried at last. "Why the devil should I be married just to please the Queen?"

Even as he spoke, however, he knew the answer only too well.

What had happened nearly two years ago at Windsor Castle he had hoped by now had been forgotten.

He had been invited to stay for a formal ball that was being given for an important visiting Royalty.

He had not been particularly excited by the invitation, knowing that the protocol at Windsor could be extremely tiresome. He would much rather be with his many friends in London or at his house in the country.

However, it was an invitation that he could not possibly refuse.

He had accordingly arrived with his valet, his groom and a team drawing his carriage.

He knew with certanty that his horses would be superior to any that would be quartered in the Royal stables.

The Queen, who liked handsome men around her, had received him more genially than she had a number of her other guests.

There was the usual audience at which nobody was allowed to sit.

It was followed by a long-drawn-out dinner where everyone spoke in lowered voices.

After that came the ball, which was a comparatively small one and the guests danced to what the Marquis considered was an inferior orchestra.

He was bored, exceedingly bored.

Then he discovered that one of the Queen's Ladies-in-Waiting, who was new, was rather attractive.

Lady Mentmore was the second wife of one of the Gentlemen-at-Arms and he had married her because he needed an heir.

In consequence he had chosen someone young, healthy and very pretty.

The Marquis danced with her twice more than the Queen would have considered conventional.

He had then suggested that he should say 'goodnight' to her later.

Lady Mentmore shook her head.

"It is too dangerous," she murmured.

"'Nothing ventured, nothing gained' is my motto," the Marquis replied.

She laughed at him provocatively and he thought again that she was very pretty and very desirable.

"Tell me where you are sleeping," he persisted.

"You could never find it," she answered. "We are tucked away and, as the place is like a rabbit warren, you would get lost and, if you are not careful, might end up in Her Majesty's bedroom!"

They both chuckled at the very idea.

Finally the Marquis persuaded Lady Mentmore to meet him on a landing that was situated somewhere between their two rooms.

He would then take her to his.

"You are quite right," he said to her, "the place is a rabbit warren and so we must take no chances of getting lost."

She was listening to him wide-eyed and he went on,

"I have been told the story a hundred times about the Ambassador who found it impossible to find his own room and slept on a sofa only to be accused by a nosey chambermaid the next day of having been too drunk to find his way to bed!"

Lady Mentmore had indeed heard the story before but she giggled attractively and the Marquis had felt that he would definitely enjoy kissing her rosebud lips.

It seemed a long time before the party ended and the Queen and her guests retired to bed.

The Marquis was installed in the oldest part of Windsor Castle.

The walls were thick and the passages narrow, where nothing said was likely to be overheard.

At one o'clock in the morning, as had been arranged with her, he found his way back to the landing and waited for Lady Mentmore.

He had been there for about five minutes when she appeared.

She was looking very lovely in a silk *negligée* trimmed with lace and her long fair hair fell over her shoulders.

There was no need for words and the Marquis put out his hand to draw her towards him.

Even as he did so, at that very moment a door opened quite near to them.

Someone peeped out and the door was closed again quickly.

Lady Mentmore, who had her back to it, was unaware of what had happened.

But the Marquis as he guided her towards his room was somewhat perturbed.

He knew only too well exactly how gossip could sweep through Windsor Castle like a North wind.

He had no idea who else might be sleeping in that part of The Castle, nor whether it was a man or a woman who had seen him with Lady Mentmore.

Anyway he told himself philosophically that it was done now.

To send her back to her bedroom would not at all mend matters and he could only hope that the person who had peeped out was of no consequence.

Lady Mentmore had more than exceeded his expectations he was delighted to recall.

But the Marquis had thought after that visit that the Queen was slightly stiffer than she had been previously.

There was a disapproving look in her eyes that had not been there before.

Now he understood that he was being punished for what had been a brief but pleasant interlude in a dull visit.

He had not been to Windsor Castle again.

So he had not come into contact with Lady Mentmore since she had left him in the early hours of the morning.

"I cannot understand, Denzil," the Lord Chamberlain was saying, "what you might have done to incur the Queen's displeasure, but, as you know only too well, nothing will stop women from gossiping."

That was indeed true.

The Marquis, however, was very well aware that, quite apart from Lady Mentmore, his reputation was not one to commend itself in any way to the Queen.

It was certainly no worse than that of her son, but Her Majesty was known to disapprove of everything that the Prince of Wales did.

"Does this mean that I shall have to be married before I can be appointed?" he now asked Lord Latham.

"Or engaged," the Lord Chamberlain said, "but I think I should warn you that Her Majesty will not leave the position vacant for very long."

"What do you mean by *very long*?" the Marquis enquired.

"Shall we say two months?" the Lord Chamberlain replied. "That will take you to approximately the middle of June."

He saw the dismay on the Marquis's face and added,

"I am sorry, Denzil. I know that this is a blow to you. At the same time you have to marry sooner or later. Your father made the mistake of having only two children and, if you would take my advice, you will fill what I am sure are the very large nurseries at Rock Park with a number of them."

The Marquis rose to his feet.

"I loathe the idea of marriage," he said angrily. "I know that any young unfledged girl, who would have the approval of Her Majesty the Queen, would bore me to distraction!"

He walked across to the window as he spoke.

There was an expression of considerable compassion in the Lord Chamberlain's eyes as he watched him,

He had been young and dashing himself and he had enjoyed the favours of a number of women before he married so he knew exactly what the Marquis was feeling.

"The Season has just started," he said aloud. "There will be many pretty girls coming to London. Some of them have already arrived. If you attend the first drawing room, you will be able to take your pick."

"I would much rather choose a horse at Tattersalls or in the Spring Sales," the Marquis snapped. "At least I would not have to be totally encumbered with it for the rest of my life!"

The Lord Chamberlain sighed and declared,

"You could, of course, refuse the position as your father did."

"What excuse could I make?" the Marquis enquired. "At least my father was a sick man. Even so there was a huge outcry amongst the family."

He walked across the room before he went on,

"I myself have no such excuse, except that I have no wish to be leg-shackled or forced to choose a wife who the Queen would approve of."

"She will, of course, be by tradition a Lady-of-the-Bedchamber," the Lord Chamberlain remarked.

"That is exactly what I mean," the Marquis replied savagely. "The Queen's choice of a Lady-of-the-Bedchamber is just not someone I am likely to find very exciting in the long winter evenings!"

"Come on now, Denzil, it is not at all as bad as that," the Lord Chamberlain said. "After all young girls, however gauche they may seem when they first appear as *debutantes*, do eventually become the polished, sophisticated exotic women you have been spending your time with ever since I can remember."

"But I have not had to marry any of them!" the Marquis pointed out.

As he spoke, he thought that, if he was married, he would very much dislike knowing that his wife was having an *affaire de coeur* with somebody like himself.

It was something that had never entered his mind until now. He had always assumed that his wife would take the place of his mother as the charming and delightful chatelaine of Rock Park.

She would adore him as his mother had adored his father to the exclusion of any other man.

He walked back from the window, knowing full well that the Lord Chamberlain was awaiting his decision, and no doubt hoping that he would not take too long about it.

Outside the sun was shining and the Marquis suddenly felt that he must go to the country. Maybe at Rock Park he would be able to think the problem over without being so angry and resentful.

For the moment he felt as if he was being encased between walls and they were gradually closing in on him and becoming a prison.

"You say I have two months," he now said aloud. "Very well, my Lord, you shall have my decision as soon as it is possible to give it to you with, I would suppose, the name of the woman I shall marry."

He spoke bitterly and the Lord Chamberlain said in a quiet voice,

"That, I am afraid, is what Her Majesty will expect."

"I am only surprised," the Marquis replied scathingly, "that she does not choose my wife for me and leave me nothing to do except put the ring on her finger!"

"I am sorry, Denzil, very sorry and, if I could have prevented this from happening, I would have for I knew how much it would upset you."

"It is most certainly not your fault," the Marquis said, "but I have always believed it is a mistake to have a woman on the Throne rather than a man!"

Because he could not help himself, the Earl laughed.

"Quite a number of people have no doubt thought that at one time or another and yet you have to admit that the Queen has made Great Britain the most powerful country in the world."

He paused a moment and then continued,

"You have only to look at your map to know that every day the areas coloured red to signify British rule increase and multiply!"

"I know, I do know," the Marquis said testily, "but when one is affected personally it becomes hard to flagwave with any enthusiasm."

Lord Chamberlain rose and came round from behind his desk.

"Cheer up," he urged. "It may not be as bad as you anticipate. I suppose it is too early to offer you a drink?"

"To drown my sorrows or to celebrate?" the Marquis enquired. "Thank you, but it is too early for either."

He put out his hand.

"Thank you, my Lord, for breaking it all to me as kindly as you could. I now have two months, nine weeks, sixty-one days of freedom left. What is more I have to spend them looking for the bait that will have me caught, hook, line and sinker for the rest of my life!"

The Lord Chamberlain laughed again.

"Whatever else you have not lost your sense of humour," he said. "If there is anything I can do to help you, please let me know."

"You have already done more than enough to help," the Marquis answered.

The Lord Chamberlain was not certain whether the Marquis was being sarcastic or grateful.

The Marquis picked up his top hat, which he had placed on a chair when he had first entered the room.

"Two months!" he muttered as if to remind himself.

Then he went from the room, closing the door quietly behind him.

The Lord Chamberlain sighed and sat down again at his desk. He knew that what he had told the Marquis had been a body blow to him.

He had admired, as everyone else did, his many achievements and above all his success with horseflesh.

However envious and jealous any man might be, he never denied that the Marquis rode magnificently.

The horses that were trained under him had all done well in many races including the Classics like the Gold Cup.

He could produce the finest horses to be seen on the Racecourse or in the hunting field.

It would be impossible, the Lord Chamberlain knew, to appoint anyone else as the Master of the Horse, who could be in any way the Marquis's equal.

He did know, however, that whatever his opinion might be on the matter, it would be impossible to change the Queen's mind.

He had daringly remonstrated with her already when she had told him the condition for the appointment.

"But the Marquis of Rockingdale, ma'am, is only twenty-eight," he had argued, "and many men settle down much later than that."

"I am well aware of that, Lord Chamberlain," the Queen replied sharply, "but the Marquis needs the steadying influence of a wife and that is something that he most certainly lacks at the moment."

The Lord Chamberlain had no idea what could have happened or why Her Majesty had taken up this attitude.

He just knew that it would be purposeless for him to try to discuss the matter further.

He therefore bowed himself gracefully out of the room wishing that somebody else had to break the disturbing news to the Marquis.

*

As the Marquis drove away from St. James's Palace, he could feel his fury rising within him.

How dare the Queen interfere in his private life!

How dare she insist upon his being married when he had no desire to make any woman his wife?

Of course, as the Lord Chamberlain had told him, he could refuse the position. To do so, however, would inevitably cause a great deal of negative comment.

Everybody would speculate as to what he had done to upset the Queen.

His whole family would take it as an insult to them personally.

Too late, as many a man had done before him, he wished that he could turn back the clock.

He greatly wished that he had not tried to alleviate the boredom of Windsor Castle by pursuing the pretty Lady Mentmore.

But what was done was done and now there was really no choice for him to make.

He had to find himself a wife and he had two months to do it in.

As he drove up St. James's Street, he was staring straight ahead of him, ignoring the raised hands of several of his friends.

He ignored too the inviting smile of a lady he passed in her open carriage.

He next drove down Piccadilly feeling oblivious of everything but his own dark thoughts.

When he reached Rock House in Park Lane, he decided that he must have time to think.

He realised only too well when he went into his study that there would be the usual pile of invitations lying on his desk.

As a rule he accepted only two or three of these and his secretary refused the rest.

Now he told himself savagely that, if he was to meet the type of lady who the Queen would approve of, he must attend the fashionable balls held practically every night in the London Season.

There waiting for him would be a bevy of *debutantes*.

At the parties he usually attended there were no ambitious Mamas speculating as to which partner their darling daughters danced with would make them suitable husbands.

They would be determining which of them was the most eligible with the best and most prestigious title.

Alternatively sufficient wealth, possessions and stately houses to keep their daughters in the manner that they were accustomed to.

No, the parties he went to were strictly for married women.

The Marquis could never remember having met a *debutante*.

Occasionally he had seen some of them sitting meekly beside their chaperones.

They would be eyeing every man who came near them, hoping that he would ask them to dance.

'They will be heavy on their feet and quite incapable of saying one intelligent word!' the Marquis thought to himself savagely.

He then picked up the gold bell that stood on his desk and rang it furiously.

When a footman opened the door, he ordered sharply,

"Send Mr. Benson to me!"

When his secretary, whom he had engaged when he succeeded on his father's death, came hurrying in he said,

"I am going to the country, Benson. Cancel all my invitations for the next few days and inform anybody who enquires that I have had to leave London on urgent family business."

That was the light word for it he thought angrily.

'Family business' that involved taking on a wife and eventually a family he did not want.

After a hasty luncheon, when he found it very difficult to swallow anything, despite the fact that his chef had prepared some of his most favourite dishes, he left Rock House.

As he climbed into his travelling chariot, the servants looked at him apprehensively.

His grooms exchanged glances as he drove his team faster than he habitually did, yet still with the expertise that he became famous for.

He actually reached Rock Park in record time.

For the very first time since he had inherited, he felt no thrill of excitement as he went up the drive.

Nor did the beauty of the great building stir his heart as it usually did.

The reason why the Marquis had spent so much time in London after growing up was not entirely because of all the attractive women who abounded there.

It was also because he found it just more and more impossible to accept the way that his father's estate was being managed.

He had served two years in the Household Cavalry after leaving Cambridge University.

He had then thought that his father would want him to take over the running of the estate and he had hoped that he would be allowed to introduce many innovations and new methods of agriculture.

He considered that these were essential improvements to be made and long overdue.

Unfortunately, however, the Marquis's father had no intention of allowing what he called 'new-fangled ideas' to change in any way his life at Rock Park.

His son had tried to persuade him that the stables were old and in need of repair.

It would be better to demolish them and build new ones with the latest system of ventilation and other modernisation.

His father had been horrified at the idea.

"They were good enough for my father and indeed for his father before him," he insisted, "and they are good enough for me."

It was the same objection he had made to every one of his son's suggestions.

Finally he became so frustrated that he went back to London.

He soon found that when not in London he could spend time very pleasantly in Leicestershire.

He owned there a comfortable Hunting Lodge where there was plenty of room for his friends.

There was a very charming house in Newmarket as well where he could supervise his racehorses. His father had made those over to him when he was twenty-one.

Each time he visited Rock Park it annoyed him more and more that it was so behind the times.

He could not understand why his father not only tolerated all these deficiencies but clung to them.

For the two years since he had inherited he had been exclusively occupied in putting into operation all the innovations that he had been longing to make.

So he had had no time for social contacts with his neighbours nor was he in any way concerned with what was happening in the County.

He was instead intent upon installing electric light in the house.

He was building new stables and organising a much better system of farming the land that was not let out to tenants but managed by the owner of Rock Park.

He pensioned off the farmer who had obeyed without questioning everything that the Marquis's father had told him to do.

This had amounted to two words, 'no change'.

He replaced him with a young man who believed in fertilisers and the rotation of crops and who was prepared to experiment freely with livestock.

The Marquis was interested in bringing in new breeds of sheep and he bred better cattle than there had ever been on his father's land.

It all took time and it meant building new cottages for the old employees he had retired and for the new workers he took on.

The Marquis enjoyed every minute of it and few people outside the estate had any idea of what he was doing.

For he had no intention of acknowledging that his father had made many costly mistakes.

In that particular part of the country the Marquis was very like a Sovereign in his own right. In point of fact Rock Park was a State within a State.

Over two thousand people were paid on Fridays for their work in the various departments of the estate, some old and some new.

The stonemasons, the bricklayers, the painters and carpenters had always been on the estate, but their numbers had gradually dwindled. Now each one of these departments was seething with young people.

They were anxious to contribute new ideas and to work the new methods that their employer demanded.

It was, the Marquis thought, the most exciting adventure that he had ever embarked on.

What he did not want was to have to share it with some tiresome young woman, who would always be thinking of herself and nothing or no one else.

She would not have the least understanding why he should exert himself in this manner.

He was dreading the very idea of her as he drove up the drive.

He was welcomed home by Dawson the butler, who had been the butler at Rock Park ever since he was a boy.

Walking across the Great Hall, the Marquis told himself that this was his, every inch of it.

Why should he want anything more?

To hell with the position of Master of the Horse!

His own horses were far finer than any in the Royal stables.

He could be content to let Her Majesty look after her own animals without any help from him.

Then he knew that, wonderful though Rock Park was, it was not enough for him.

He wanted more, much more.

He wanted the power that was part of the Monarchy. The power to contribute to the Nation by improving first of all the horses in the Royal stables.

Then perhaps he would serve England in some other capacity in which only he could excel.

'I have to do it, *I have to*!' he told himself.

But he knew with a sinking of his heart that he was not permitted to do it alone.

*

The Marquis spent a surprisingly peaceful night.

He had expected to be awake worrying over his future. Instead, because he had already stressed himself out, he slept until dawn.

He had told his valet to call him early, but he was up and half-dressed before the man appeared.

"You're right early, my Lord," the valet remarked.

"I have a great deal to do," the Marquis replied.

The most important thing that he had to do, he told himself, was something that he did not want to even think about.

The valet knew that his Master would want breakfast earlier than expected, so he quickly sent a footman to warn the chef.

By the time the Marquis entered the breakfast room there were six entrée dishes already on the sideboard and Dawson was carrying in the silver coffee pot.

He had known the Marquis long enough to realise that something was wrong.

He was therefore aware that it would be a mistake to be talkative and he certainly must not ask the Marquis questions.

He put the silver coffee pot down in front of the Marquis, who was sitting at the head of the table, and then left the room.

Breakfast was the one meal when the servants of the house did not wait at table.

This was an old tradition, the Marquis thought, that should not be changed. He so much preferred helping himself and being able to read the newspaper without having to put up with anyone moving about in the room and asking stupid questions.

He was therefore surprised as he started to eat a dish of kidneys and mushrooms when he heard the door open behind him.

"Excuse me, my Lord," Dawson said, "But Lady Athina Ling has called."

"At this hour?" the Marquis exclaimed.

He then tried to remember who Lady Athina Ling was. The name seemed to ring a bell, but for the moment he could not recall her.

"Lady Athina," Dawson said respectfully, "is the daughter of the late Earl of Murling whose estate marches with your Lordship's."

"Oh, yes, of course," the Marquis answered.

"Her Ladyship apologises to you for disturbing you so early in the morning, my Lord, but she says it's on a very urgent matter."

The Marquis decided immediately that it would be rude to send her away.

He therefore replied,

"Tell Lady Athina that I will see her as soon as I have finished my breakfast, but I am in fact going riding."

"I'll inform her Ladyship," Dawson replied and left.

The Marquis deliberately went over to the sideboard and poured himself another cup of coffee.

'What can the damned woman want at this hour of the morning?' he fumed to himself.

He wanted to ride over his own land on his own horse and try to clear his thoughts in the fresh air

He did not want to talk to anybody, he just wanted to think.

He had nevertheless the most uncomfortable feeling that, however much he thought about the dilemma that he was facing, there was no solution.

CHAPTER FOUR

Only as she walked up the steps to the front door of Rock Park with Peter holding her hand tightly did Athina realise that it was much too early for anyone to be making a call on anyone.

She had been so afraid that Lord Burnham might overtake her on the road and snatch Peter away from her.

She had thought of nothing but reaching Rock Park as a haven of safety.

The door was then opened promptly by a footman and, when she and Peter entered the hall, a grey-haired butler came forward.

"I should be grateful if I could see the Marquis of Rockingdale immediately," she asked. "It is on a very urgent matter."

Thinking that the butler looked slightly sceptical, she continued,

"I am Lady Athina Ling."

The butler's face lit up and he said,

"Of course, my Lady. I well remember the late Earl coming here often."

He went ahead and showed her into a study.

There were some fine pictures of horses by Stubbs on the walls and the room contained comfortable masculine furniture all covered in red leather.

The butler went out of the room and Peter asked,

"Is it my uncle who we are going to see? I don't think I remember him."

"I would expect you will when you see him again," Athina said confidently.

She nearly added,

'He must have been at your mother's funeral,' and then thought that it might upset Peter.

Instead she went on,

"This is a beautiful house and I am sure that your mother loved playing in these big rooms when she was a little girl."

"She used to tell me about the swing in the garden and a little house in the trees," Peter said as if he were just recalling it.

The butler came back to say,

"His Lordship'll see you, my Lady, as soon as he's finished his breakfast."

"Thank you," Athina replied, "and, as I would like to speak to him alone, I wonder if it would be at all possible to give Lady Louise's son, Peter, who is here with me, something to eat? We have come a long way and I am sure that he is both hungry and thirsty."

"Master Peter!" the butler exclaimed. "I wondered who the young gentleman was and thought he resembled someone I knew. Of course, it's Lady Louise!"

He was obviously pleased at meeting Peter and then, putting out his hand, he suggested,

"If you'll come with me now, Master Peter, I'll give you some breakfast and show you the secret safe in my pantry that your mother used to love when she was your age."

Peter looked interested.

"Why is it a secret?" he wanted to know.

They went from the room and Athina could hear the butler telling Peter about the silver safe as they went down the passage.

She walked over to the window to look out at the lake a little way below the house.

She could see swans and ducks swimming in it and beyond it in the Park that they had just driven through was a herd of spotted deer.

It was all so beautiful and looked so peaceful.

It seemed really incredible that one of the family, so young and so vulnerable, should be treated in such a horrifying manner.

The door opened and the Marquis came in.

Athina turned around slowly.

She thought at a quick first glance that he was younger and more handsome than she might have anticipated.

She had no idea that the Marquis was astonished at her looks and she was so very different from what he had expected.

He walked across the room and held out his hand.

"How do you do, Lady Athina. I don't think we have ever met but I remember your father well. And I was extremely sorry to learn of his death."

"As you can imagine, I miss him very much," Athina replied.

"So what can I do for you?" the Marquis asked in a brisk tone. "I expect that Dawson, my butler, has told you that I was just about to go riding."

"I would not have called so early," Athina explained, "if it had not been of the utmost importance that directly concerns your nephew, Peter Naver."

The Marquis looked surprised.

"What has he been up to?" he asked. "And how does it concern you?"

Athina sat down on a sofa that stood next to the fireplace.

"Last night," she began, "I had to stay at a Posting inn called *The Crown and Feathers*. While I was having dinner, I noticed at a table close to me a gentleman who was being noisily aggressive to a small boy."

"You were staying alone?" the Marquis queried unexpectedly.

"I had had a slight accident to the wheel of my chaise," Athina replied, "and was unable to proceed until early this morning."

She thought that his interruption was unnecessary and went on,

"I was just going to sleep in my bedroom when I heard a small boy, who I afterwards learnt was your nephew, screaming in the next room."

The Marquis frowned.

"Why was he screaming?"

"He was screaming," Athina replied, "because his stepfather, who I understand, is Lord Burnham, was furious because he had gone to the stables to comfort a horse that Lord Burnham had whipped on the journey."

She then paused a moment and this time the Marquis did not say anything,

"To punish him," Athina continued, "he whipped the poor boy unmercifully until he was almost unconscious."

There was silence as the Marquis stared at Athina as if he could hardly credit what she was saying.

Then he commented,

"I cannot believe that my brother-in-law could be so cruel as you imply. After all small boys often require correction. There is nothing unusual about their being spanked."

"This was no question of being spanked," Athina replied sharply. "He was beaten unmercifully with a whip that left open weals on his skin."

The Marquis walked across the room to his desk and then back again before he said,

"I quite understand, Lady Athina, that you were upset but I assure you most boys do get whipped at some time or another. I have always believed that my nephew is being well looked after by his stepfather. So it would be incorrect for me to interfere in his upbringing."

Athina rose to her feet.

She was thinking that her father had been right in everything he had said about the Marquis.

She had slept very little last night and was tired from the journey and now she felt her temper rising.

She did not speak, however, but walked towards the door.

"Where are you going?" the Marquis asked as she reached it.

Athina turned back.

"As you have lived up to your reputation, my Lord," she said, "I will tell you exactly what I am doing. I am taking Peter to Windsor Castle. I will show the Queen how brutally a Peer of the Realm has marked the child and will warn her that her new Master of the Horse is likely to treat Her Majesty's own horses in the same manner."

If she had thrown a bomb at the Marquis, he could not have been more surprised.

Never in his whole life had a woman spoken to him in such a way.

It seemed incredible that anyone so small, so fragile and beautiful, should so insult him in his own house.

Athina started to open the door.

The Marquis then realised abruptly that she would undoubtedly do what she had threatened.

She would indeed go to Windsor Castle and he was well aware of the damage it would cause him.

Quickly he turned and walked swiftly towards her saying,

"Forgive me, Lady Athina, if I sounded in any way callous. Of course I am concerned about my sister's child."

Athina stood still, but she did not speak and he said again,

"Please forgive me and let's discuss this sensibly. I am convinced now that you are not exaggerating the situation, as I had first thought."

Slowly and somewhat reluctantly Athina closed the door and she then turned back into the room.

As she did so, she looked at the Marquis and he knew that he had never seen a woman look at him with such contempt. j

He found it hard to believe that she disliked him as much as she appeared to do.

"Come and sit down," he proposed in his most engaging tone.

Again slowly, as if she was only half-persuaded to do so, Athina walked back to the place that she had vacated on the sofa.

"Now let's start from the beginning," the Marquis suggested, "and try to forget that I said all the wrong things and so upset you."

He had never met a woman who did not succumb to his charm when he pleaded with her.

He was aware, however, that Athina was sitting very straight and stiff on the edge of the sofa.

He could feel her hostility vibrating from her.

"Let me explain to you," the Marquis continued, "that when my sister died she left her son in the charge of her second husband, Lord Burnham."

Athina made no comment and he went on,

"In fact she made a will, leaving her money, which amounted to a considerable sum, since she had a large private fortune left to her by her Godfather, to Peter with Lord Burnham as the Administrator of it until Peter reached the age of twenty-one."

He paused and then added as if he was trying to remember the exact wording that had been used,

"If anything happened to Peter before then, the money was to go to Lord Burnham and not back to the mother's family as might have been expected."

Now he made a little gesture with his hand before he said,

"You can understand why I was not concerned in any way as to where my nephew lived or what he did. Nor have any of my relatives, who have seen him, made any complaints as to the way he is being treated."

Even as he spoke the Marquis remembered something.

Someone had told him that Lord Burnham had been short of cash before his wife died.

Perhaps it was a chance remark because he could not recall who had said it. Nor had it made any real impact on him at the time.

Now, however, it now struck him that it was, of course, extremely convenient for his brother-in-law to have the care of a child who was so rich.

There was still no response from Athina to what he had just said.

So after a moment the Marquis went on,

"I will, of course, speak directly to Lord Burnham and tell him of your complaint and we can only hope that he will be kinder to the boy in the future."

"I heard the way that Lord Burnham was behaving last night," Athina said slowly, "and I would not allow any child, not even one who is older and stronger than Peter, to be in that brute's care for another five minutes!"

She drew in her breath before she added,

"I brought Peter here to you because I thought that you would save him and protect him. If you refuse to do anything, then I will! Even if it means taking Peter to Windsor Castle or going abroad with him."

The Marquis looked bewildered.

"I don't quite understand. Are you saying that you have brought the boy here to me?"

"I thought that your butler would have told you," Athina said. "I smuggled him away at five o'clock this morning. We have driven at great speed because I was afraid that Lord Burnham would overtake me and snatch Peter away from me."

She saw that the Marquis was still looking somewhat puzzled and she explained,

"We had no time for breakfast and, as I wanted to speak to you alone, your butler has taken Peter to have something to eat."

"In that case before we go any further I would like to meet my nephew."

Athina rose from the sofa with her head held high and then the Marquis hurried to open the door for her.

She was disliking him intensely for not being appalled by this obvious cruelty to a child.

They walked down the corridor towards the hall.

The Marquis was wondering where Dawson had taken the boy when the butler appeared.

"If you're looking for Master Peter, my Lady," he said to Athina, "I gave him some breakfast, but he couldn't eat much because his back was hurting him. So I've taken him upstairs to Mrs. Field. She'll know what to do."

"Mrs. Field is my housekeeper," the Marquis explained.

"Thank you," Athina said to the butler, "I would like to go up to him."

"I will take you," the Marquis suggested.

They walked up the impressive staircase side by side in silence.

When they reached the first floor, the Marquis turned left and they walked a long way down a wide corridor.

He then opened a door that was covered in green baize, which Athina knew would lead into the servants' part of the house.

After they had passed through it, he opened another door on the right hand side of the corridor.

They walked into a sitting room where the sunshine was pouring in through tall windows.

Peter was standing in front of one of the windows in his trousers and without his shirt.

An elderly woman with a kind face was examining his back.

When he saw Athina come into the room, Peter gave a cry and ran to her.

He held out his arms and Athina went down on her knees and, as he flung himself against her, she pulled off her hat so that it was easier to kiss him.

He put his arms round her neck and his cheek against hers.

"I thought – you had – gone – away," he stuttered.

"No, no, of course, I would not do that," Athina comforted him. "I am here and I understand your back is hurting you."

"It itched – and – itched," Peter said. "I wanted to – scratch it but I – could not – reach."

As he spoke, Athina heard Mrs. Field saying to the Marquis,

"Never in all me born years, my Lord, have I seen anythin' so wicked and horrible as the way this poor little boy's been treated. It be enough to make her Ladyship turn in her grave!"

The Marquis had moved round so that he could see Peter's back where the light from the window shone on it.

If anything it looked worse than it had last night and during the long drive several of the weals had bled and had stuck to his shirt.

The skin surrounding them was red and swollen.

He could also see what Athina had seen that there were old scars still on his back from previous beatings.

"You will – not leave me – will – you?" Peter was asking her desperately.

He was almost in tears and speaking in a whisper, but the Marquis heard.

"I promise you I will not," Athina assured him, "but you must let this kind lady put some cream on your back, which I should have done this morning. It was stupid of me not to, but I was in such a hurry to get away."

"We escaped – from Step-Papa," Peter murmured.

"Yes, we escaped," Athina agreed.

"And you don't – think – Step-Papa will find – me here?"

There was a note of terror in Peter's voice.

Athina looked up at the Marquis who was standing behind him.

"I can answer that question," the Marquis asserted, "and I promise you that your stepfather will never beat you again."

There was a hard note in his voice. If there was one thing that the Marquis loathed above everything else it was cruelty.

He had once knocked a man down on the Racecourse for beating a horse that had not won a race that he had been expected to win.

And he had been challenged by a member of White's Club to a duel because he had accused him of ill-treating one of his carriage horses.

The Marquis saw Athina's eyes light up as if the sunshine was bursting through the gloom.

It suddenly struck him that kneeling on the floor with Peter's arms around her, she looked very lovely.

With her head close to Peter's she might have stepped down from a picture painted by a great Master of the Madonna and Child.

After he had spoken, Peter loosened his tight hold on Athina and he turned his face round to look at the Marquis.

"This is your uncle," Athina then told him. "He knows that we ran away and I have brought you here for his protection."

She looked at the Marquis quizzically as she spoke.

The Marquis held out his hand.

"I am delighted to meet you, Peter and I think it was very clever of you to run away with Lady Athina. Now I have to talk to her about what we are going to do in the future."

"I will – not have – to go – back to Step-Papa – will I?" Peter asked in a quavering voice.

"I promise you that you will not have to," the Marquis replied.

He looked at Mrs. Field.

"Now suppose you work your magic on Master Peter's back," he said, "while I take her Ladyship downstairs to have some breakfast."

"I'll do that, my Lord," Mrs. Field said. "I've already promised the young gentleman that he'll feel quite different when I've put some honey on his wound."

"Honey!" Athina exclaimed. "Will that take away the pain?"

"He'll have no pain and these terrible scars will heal in two days," Mrs. Field assured her.

"I have never heard of anybody using honey before".

"My Ma were known as 'the white witch'," Mrs. Field answered, "and people come from far and wide to get the herbal remedies she made for 'em. But she always said that when it come to healin' cuts there's nothin' like honeys and I always uses it meself."

"What do you think of that, Peter?" the Marquis exclaimed. "You have a white witch looking after you. And who could ask for more?"

Peter looked at Mrs. Field wide-eyed.

"Do you fly on a broomstick?" he then asked her.

"I wishes I could," she replied. "That's what they used to say me Ma did and that's what you'll want to do when your back's healed. So come on and let me put some honey on it."

Athina rose to her feet.

"Stay with Mrs. Field until she has finished," she advised him, "and I will be downstairs waiting for you."

Peter put out his hand to touch her.

"You – promise? You will not go – away without – me?"

"I promise," Athina said after another glance at the Marquis.

She picked up her hat which she had put down on a chair.

Then she said to Mrs. Field,

"Thank you, thank you very much. I am very grateful for all your help with poor Peter."

She saw that Mrs. Field was about to put what looked like thick clover honey on strips of linen and they would cover Peter's injuries and held in place by a bandage.

The Marquis opened the door and they then walked out into the corridor.

She thought that he would say something to her, but they went on in silence down the stairs and into the breakfast room.

Dawson must have anticipated that this was what they would do and he was just placing a silver coffee pot on a tray at the top of the table.

"You say you left at five o'clock," the Marquis said. "You must be really starving by now."

"I admit to feeling a trifle hungry," Athina replied, "but usually one becomes thirsty when driving because of the dust."

She remembered as she was speaking how Peter had said that his stepfather would not let him stop for a drink of water yesterday.

She felt that there was no point in giving further instances to the Marquis of the cruelty that the child had suffered. It was enough that the Marquis had seen his back.

He walked over to the sideboard and lifted the lids of some of the entrée dishes.

"Will you have eggs or fish or both?" he asked her.

Athina gave a little laugh.

"I think a little of both would be very nice, my Lord."

She sat down at the table and he brought two plates to her.

Then he poured out some coffee into a cup for her and another for himself saying as he did so,

"There is no need for me to admit in words that I was wrong and that you were absolutely right."

"I thought you would agree with me when you saw for yourself what has been happening to Peter," Athina said. "I suppose it would have been more sensible to let you see him first."

She thought that they were each conceding something to the other.

Her common sense told her that, if she was to fight for Peter, it was essential to have the Marquis on her side.

He was obviously thinking and she remained silent until he said,

"Do you think Burnham will follow you?"

"I was thinking on the way here that he would," Athina answered, "once he realised that there was a communicating door between my room and Peter's. He had locked Peter's outside door so he would know that Peter must have left with me."

She paused for a moment before she added,

"He will learn that I left very early in the morning, but he will not know who I am."

"Why is that?" the Marquis asked.

"Because I gave the proprietor the name of my chaperone, Mrs. Beckwith," Athina explained.

She hesitated for a moment before she went on,

"But my groom was in my father's livery and there were other grooms there who might have recognised it."

The Marquis nodded.

"I should think it would be more than likely. Burnham, who has, of course, often stayed here at Rock Park might well be aware that our estates march with each other."

Athina stiffened.

"In which case he will go straight to Murling Park. What shall I – do? What shall I – say if he – comes?"

She suddenly felt rather helpless.

Her servants were old and she remembered how aggressive and loud-voiced Lord Burnham had been.

She felt sure that she and Mrs. Beckwith would not be able to cope with him.

She was suddenly frightened.

So frightened that she forgot for a moment or two her dislike of the Marquis and said pleadingly,

"I promised Peter that he would not have to go – back with Lord Burnham and also that I would not – leave him. Tell me what I should do – *please – tell me*."

"Peter will stay here," the Marquis said firmly, "and I will cope with Burnham. At the same time, as I am an unmarried man, there is every possibility that he will assert I am not a suitable person to be in charge of a child."

As he spoke the word 'unmarried', the Marquis had an idea.

For the moment it seemed so inconceivable that he could hardly formulate it to himself.

Then, as he tried to do so, the door opened and Peter came in. He was not wearing a coat, but he had on a clean white shirt.

Athina guessed that Mrs. Field had found a shirt that had once belonged to the Marquis when he was a small boy.

Peter walked towards her saying,

"My back – feels better – much – much better – already."

He went to stand beside Athina's chair and looked at what was on her plate.

"The butler told me that you ate very little at breakfast," Athina said, "and now that you are feeling better, perhaps you would like some more?"

"Can I have some more?" Peter asked. "Step-Papa never allowed me to have a second helping and, when he says I have been naughty, I have no food for a whole day."

"That must make you feel very hungry," Athina remarked.

"I have a big hole in my tummy," Peter replied, "and sometimes I feel so weak it's difficult to get out of bed."

Athina looked at the Marquis.

Although it seemed strange, she realised that she could read his thoughts.

They were both thinking the same thing and it was so incredible that she almost dismissed it as pure imagination.

She just knew, however, beyond any doubt that the same idea had occurred to Peter's uncle.

"Well, Peter, now that you are here with me," the Marquis said aloud, "you are to eat big meals every day, otherwise you will not be strong enough to ride my horses."

"Ride your horses?" Peter repeated. "Can I really?"

"Of course you can, Peter," the Marquis promised. "Your father was a very good rider and I expect you are too."

He rose from the table as he spoke and lifted the lids of the entrée dishes in the same way that he had for Athina and this time he lifted more of them.

"Now you have to eat all this," he said to Peter, "and, if this is not enough, we will tell the chef to make you some more."

Peter laughed.

"If I eat all that I will get so fat that I will be – too heavy for your horses to carry me!"

"We will risk it," the Marquis replied, "and, if my horses cannot manage you, we will try the ones that draw the carts."

Peter laughed as if it was a huge joke.

Athina thought that the Marquis at least was clever in gaining the confidence of the small boy.

He piled Peter's plate with food and poured him out some milk and then he sat down again at the head of the table.

As he did so, Athina suggested,

"As I have finished, my Lord, I would like to have another word with you about where we should go now and what we should do."

"Yes, of course," the Marquis agreed.

Peter looked up from the other end of the table as Athina rose to her feet.

"You are – not leaving – me?" he asked in a nervous voice.

"I am just going back to the study with your uncle. I am sure that Dawson will come and tell you more about what your mother enjoyed when she was a little girl."

The Marquis had already rung the bell while Athina was speaking,

"Master Peter is very hungry, Dawson," he said. "I have told him he is to eat everything he can so that he will be strong enough to ride the biggest of my horses."

"I be sure he'll soon be riding, my Lord."

"Now see that he has everything he wants," the Marquis went on, "and, when he has finished, you can bring him to the study."

"Very good, my Lord, and I'll look after Master Peter," Dawson replied.

Athina just stopped long enough to smooth Peter's hair back and drop a kiss on his forehead.

"There is no hurry," she told him softly. "You are going to stay here and anyway I do *not* think that your stepfather will find us for a long time."

As she spoke, she felt Peter's relief as he let out a deep sigh and it seemed to seep through his small body.

She knew only too well that the child was terrified of being beaten again.

As she and the Marquis went into the study, he closed the door behind them before he began,

"I have a proposition to put to you, Lady Athina. And I only hope that it will not make you angry again."

"I am not angry now that I know you realise how much Peter has suffered and that it cannot go on," Athina replied quietly.

She was silent for a few moments and then she said in a very low voice,

"I-I knew what you were – thinking just now – and I was thinking the same thing – that his stepfather is trying to – *kill* him!"

"It did pass through my mind," the Marquis admitted. "But how could any man in his position even think of such a dreadful thing as murdering a little boy?"

"You can see how thin Peter is," Athina insisted, "and the terrible injuries that have been inflicted on his back. Not only is he terrified, but he has also been deprived of food and drink – "

"I realise that now," the Marquis interrupted, "and it makes me so angry that it would give me the greatest pleasure to give my brother-in-law a taste of his own medicine."

He spoke savagely and then in a different tone he stated,

"At the same time he is a much older man than I am and it would be a great mistake, whatever else we might do, to create any kind of a scandal."

"Are you afraid that a scandal would damage your reputation?" Athina asked him somewhat sarcastically.

"I was not actually thinking of myself," the Marquis answered, "but of my family. As you can imagine, if it becomes known what has been happening to the boy, there will be such an uproar and as his Guardian Burnham will make things more unpleasant for us than we could for him."

"I understand what you are saying," Athina replied, "but I am thinking only of Peter."

"I do have a solution to this problem and that is what I want to explain to you," the Marquis proposed.

"I am listening," Athina responded.

Next she sat down in the same place on the sofa where she had sat before with both hands in her lap.

The Marquis walked over to the fireplace and stood with his back to it

Then he said,

"If you think you have a problem, Lady Athina, so have I. What I am going to tell you is strictly confidential and I feel sure that you will not repeat it to anybody else."

Athina nodded and he went on,

"I was informed only yesterday by the Lord Chamberlain that Her Majesty the Queen will appoint me her Master of the Horse on the one condition that I am married or engaged to be."

Athina stared at him.

"But, as have I told you, I have always understood that it was a tradition that the Head of your Family should hold such a position. At least that is what my father told me some years ago."

"That is true," the Marquis agreed, "but the decision as to who occupies the post is, of course, for Her Majesty to make."

Athina wondered how this could concern Peter and then she asked him,

"What are you going to do about it, my Lord?"

"I was thinking that it might be dangerous for you to take Peter to your home, as I think you intend," the Marquis said. "He can stay here. but I think my brother-in-law will protest."

He paused a moment and then continued,

"As I am much younger than he is and, of course, unmarried, he could readily claim that he is a far more suitable Guardian for the boy than I am."

As if Athina at that moment had become suddenly aware of where the conversation was leading, she stiffened.

"What I am suggesting," the Marquis went on, "is that for Peter's sake and mine you agree to an engagement between us which – "

"No! *No!* Of course not!" Athina interrupted him. "I vowed a long time ago that I would never marry anyone unless I was in love with him! I can only say, my Lord – and I don't wish to be rude – that I would not marry you under any circumstances!"

"I have no wish to be married myself," the Marquis said, "and, if you had allowed me, Lady Athina, to finish my sentence, I was going to say that it would be 'an engagement' that we privately agree can be terminated at any time that suits either of us."

Athina stared at him.

Then she queried,

"Do you mean – it will just be a – pretence?"

"Of course that is exactly what I mean for, if you have no wish to be married, no more do I."

He looked at her a moment and then went on,

"However, to announce our engagement could make me Master of the Horse and at the same time enable you to stay here with, of course, your chaperone, until such time as Lord Burnham accepts that he is no longer Peter's Guardian."

Athina pressed her hands together.

Now she understood just what the Marquis was putting forward.

She could see that from Peter's point of view it was the only way that he could be safe and she could be with him to protect him.

As it also solved the Marquis's problem, there was no reason for her to be afraid that she would become too involved with him.

Nor was there any reason, and this was vitally important, that she might eventually be forced into marrying him.

He was watching the changing expression on her face and quite unexpectedly she then exclaimed,

"That is a very clever idea! I see now exactly what you mean and, of course, Lord Burnham could have no valid objection to your future wife wanting to have charge of Peter. Your family also will accept it as the natural thing to do."

"That is just what I thought myself," the Marquis said in a tone of some satisfaction. "Then, when the danger is past and Burnham is no longer a threat, you can say that you find me intolerable and break off the engagement, something that I would be unable to do."

"Do you really mean that I could stay here for the time being?" Athina asked eagerly.

"I should be delighted to have you as my guest with the chaperone who you said you had living with you at Murling Park."

"Mrs. Beckwith is a most charming and delightful person and a great authority on the geography of the world. I think you will find her very interesting. She is incidentally the daughter of the Bishop of Oxford."

The Marquis laughed.

"That is certainly a very good cover. It might be part of a plot in a Drury Lane drama!"

"I would almost enjoy it myself if it was not for Peter," Athina said. "You do see the terrible way that the boy has been – treated?"

Her voice broke on the last word and the Marquis expostulated,

"Only a devil could treat a small child like that! I only wish to God I had known about it earlier. I promise you, Lady Athina, I would kill that man sooner than let him touch Louise's son again."

He spoke with a sincerity that Athina just knew was genuine.

"I am sure that Peter will be very happy here," she said, "and, if we both love him, as he so wants to be loved, he will quickly forget what has happened to him this past year."

"What I really cannot understand," the Marquis said, "is why my relatives, who are usually so nosey and miss nothing of what goes on, had no idea what Burnham was like or how the child has been tortured by him."

"I think it would be a mistake to underestimate Lord Burnham," Athina suggested. "I thought he was a loud and unpleasant bully even before I heard him beating poor Peter and, if it is a question of money, which is always at the root of all evil, I think he will fight to get Peter back."

She sighed before she went on,

"He might take even more drastic steps."

"Now you are frightening me," the Marquis protested, "and I just refuse to be frightened. The man is a monster and sooner or later will get his just deserts. But meanwhile you and I have to be clever about this."

"We must certainly try."

The Marquis sat down on the sofa beside her.

"So, you agree we announce to the world, or rather to my family and the Lord Chamberlain, that we are engaged to be married."

He smiled at her before he continued,

"It will be published in *The London Gazette*. We will immediately send over to Murling Park for your chaperone and, of course, for what clothes you will require while you are staying here."

He paused for breath and then added,

"I will get my secretary to start writing at once to my relations to tell them the *good news*."

Athina was listening to him intently.

And then she said,

"I can see that you are an organiser and I am therefore content to leave these things in your hands. All I am really concerned with at the moment is to make Peter happy and to protect him from that horrible man."

She met the Marquis's eyes as she spoke.

She knew that he was thinking, as she was, that Lord Burnham would not give in easily.

CHAPTER FIVE

"Do you know, Uncle Denzil," Peter related, as they sat round the table at luncheon, "that Michelangelo was the first person to know what a horse looked like inside. He made a drawing of it."

"I suppose Mrs. Beckwith showed you that in one of the books in the library," the Marquis replied.

He looked across the table at Mrs. Beckwith and asked,

"Does that come under History or Geography?"

Mrs. Beckwith's eyes twinkled.

"It comes, my Lord, under Useful Hints for Horse Breeders."

"Breeders?" the Marquis queried.

"I am going to breed the finest horse in the world," Peter cried. "His father will be Samson and then his mother will be Aunt Athina's Juno. He will win the Grand National and I will be riding him."

The Marquis laughed.

"That is certainly an ambitious programme!"

He turned to Athina, who was sitting next to him, and said,

"You did not tell me that you owned a good breeding mare."

"I have in fact quite a number."

The Marquis raised his eyebrows.

"Why did you not tell me about them?"

"I thought," she replied, "that it would be presuming on Xanadu."

The Marquis laughed again.

"Is that how you think of Rock Park?"

"Of course," she replied, "and you are undoubtedly Kublai Khan."

"He should wear a crown," Peter said. "When Mrs. Beckwith read me the poem, I was quite sure that Kublai Khan would wear a crown."

The Marquis thought that it was all quite extraordinary.

During the last four days the conversation at meals had been full of wit and wisdom.

It was something he had never imagined could take place between two women and a small boy.

Athina had been right when she had said that Mrs. Beckwith was extremely intelligent and so indeed she was.

Peter was already a different child from how he had been on his arrival. He was eating well and spent every minute that he could in the stables with the horses.

The Marquis had to his great delight already mounted him on one of them.

He had decided that Athina and Peter would ride with him every morning either before or after breakfast.

There had been no sign at all of Lord Burnham and gradually they ceased to be tense and on edge.

Now they were all laughing.

The Marquis was teasing Peter on his intention to win the Grand National when Dawson came into the drawing room.

He walked up to the Marquis's side and said,

"Lord Burnham is here, my Lord, and I've shown him into the study."

There was a moment's complete silence.

And then Peter gave a scream of terror.

He jumped from his chair and ran to the Marquis holding onto him frantically.

"You will – not let – him take me away? Oh, please – Uncle Denzil – promise you – will not make me go – with him."

The Marquis put his arm round the boy.

"I have already promised you that," he replied in a quiet voice. "Now I want you to be brave and not make a scene, but go upstairs now with Mrs. Beckwith and stay in your sitting room until I send for you."

"You will – not listen – to him when he – tells you that I want – to be with – him like – he told Grandmama?"

"No, of course not," the Marquis answered. "You must trust me, Peter. I want you to live here with Aunt Athina and me."

Athina rose as he spoke and came around the table. Peter turned towards her and hid his face in her breast.

"I am – frightened!" he whispered, "very very – frightened!"

"You have to trust your uncle," she said soothingly.

As she spoke, she went down on her knees and held him close against her.

It was the same attitude that she had had the first morning when she and the Marquis had gone up to the housekeeper's room together.

He had thought then that she looked like a Madonna.

Now, as he saw the love in her eyes, he thought that this was how every woman should look at a child.

"You are all right, you are quite safe," Athina was saying. "Now go upstairs with Mrs. Beckwith and use the side staircase so that no one will see you."

Dawson had said that Lord Burnham was waiting in the study, but nevertheless Athina thought that it would be a mistake to take any chances.

Mrs. Beckwith put out her hand and Peter went with her. Both Athina and the Marquis knew that he was terrified and close to tears.

"Do you really want me to come with you?" Athina asked when they were alone.

"You know it is essential."

"I think I am almost as terrified as Peter," Athina said in a low voice.

"Leave everything to me," the Marquis answered.

He rose from the table and they walked slowly towards the door.

Athina thought that it was impossible for there to be so much at stake just because of one man's cruelty.

She felt that it would completely destroy Peter if his stepfather regained control of him.

It would also break her heart and Mrs. Beckwith's. She had told Athina only this morning that she had never known a more attractive and charming little boy.

"Peter is a joy to teach," she had smiled.

Besides this, Athina had the feeling that the Marquis himself was growing more and more fond of his nephew every day.

There was certainly no sign of him wishing to return to London and he spent a great deal of his time with Peter.

In the evenings the conversation between him, Mrs. Beckwith and herself was sparkling and usually very amusing.

She had to admit that it was a joy to be able to talk to the Marquis in the same way that she had always talked to her father.

He, however, was full of ideas that would never have entered the Earl's head.

It was the Marquis who had suggested that Peter should call her 'Aunt Athina'. And it made her concern for him more obvious.

At the same time they had both been aware that eventually Lord Burnham would catch up with them.

Now it had happened.

Athina felt that the ceiling had fallen in on her head and the walls were all crumbling around her.

Without speaking she and the Marquis walked towards the study and a footman opened the door for them.

The Marquis went in first.

Lord Burnham, looking large, aggressive and extremely red-faced was standing with his back to the fireplace.

He appeared somewhat debauched as if, Athina thought, he had been drinking heavily.

"Good afternoon, Roland," the Marquis began. "I rather expected that you would turn up sooner or later."

They did not shake hands and now Lord Burnham was looking at Athina.

The Marquis turned to her.

"Let me, my dear, introduce my brother-in-law, Lord Burnham," he said, "and we must ask him to congratulate us."

"Congratulate you?" Lord Burnham asked.

"Lady Athina Ling and I are engaged to be married," the Marquis explained. "The announcement of our engagement will appear in *The London Gazette* tomorrow morning."

"I have in fact been to Murling Park," Lord Burnham said, "in search of a woman called Beckwith whom I understand kidnapped my stepson when I was staying at a Posting inn."

He glowered at Athina and continued,

"But from the description I had of Mrs. Beckwith, I think now it is Lady Athina who I should have been looking for."

"I am very sorry if you were perturbed at Peter's disappearance," Athina said, "but he was very unhappy and I thought it essential that the terrible damage you had inflicted to his back should have proper attention."

"How dare you take him away from me like that!" Lord Burnham bellowed.

The Marquis held up his hand.

"Don't get into one of your rages," he admonished. "My fiancée did exactly the right thing in bringing

Peter to me. I was appalled by the terrible weals on the child's back. I simply cannot understand how you could have treated him so brutally."

"Boys need to be disciplined," Lord Burnham blustered. "If he was in as bad a way as Lady Athina thought, she should have told me what she was doing. I have had a devil of a job trying to find out what has happened to my stepson."

"How did you discover his whereabouts?" the Marquis asked in a genial tone.

As he spoke. he indicated with his right hand that Athina should sit down.

She sat on the edge of the sofa where he had first talked to her and the Marquis sat on the arm of one of the chairs. He supported himself by putting his arms across the back of it.

Athina knew, because he seemed so at ease, that Lord Burnham was slightly nonplussed.

"What I discovered," he announced, "after a great deal of trouble to myself was that my valet thought that he recognised the livery of the groom on the chaise that Peter must have been taken away in, but unfortunately it took him some time to put a name to it."

He took a deep breath before he went on,

"When finally I knew that it belonged to the late Earl of Murling, I drove to Murling Park intending to interrogate Mrs. Beckwith."

"That was when you learned that she had come here with Lady Athina as her chaperone," the Marquis said in a tone of satisfaction.

"I have come here," Lord Beckwith corrected him, "to take my stepson back to where he belongs, which is in *my* house."

"I am afraid that is quite impossible," the Marquis declared. "He is very happy and content here and my fiancée loves having him with us. "

He smiled at Athina before he went on,

"He is now being taught by Mrs. Beckwith who is one of the most intelligent women I have ever met and his back is gradually healing and returning to normal."

He said the last sentence very slowly and Lord Burnham did not meet his eyes.

"Perhaps I was a little too harsh," he admitted after a moment, "but the boy was continually disobedient and spending far much too much time with horses instead of on other things that were required of him."

"His love of horses comes naturally from his father," the Marquis replied, "and from my sister who, as you know, rode extremely well. I can imagine that nothing would please her more than that her dear son should be here with me riding my horses."

"I dispute that," Lord Burnham challenged him aggressively. "Your sister in her will left Peter in my charge and so I insist on carrying out her wishes. And I intend to have no nonsense from you or anybody else!"

Now there was a look in his eyes that told Athina that his temper was definitely rising.

"Did you really think that I would return my nephew, who is not very strong, to you to be beaten until he is almost insensible?" the Marquis asked. "If so you are very much mistaken! He is staying here with my fiancée and me and once we are married we will bring him up with our own children."

"You will do nothing of the sort!" Lord Burnham roared. "Louise gave Peter into my care and as his stepfather I am therefore his natural Guardian. If I go to Law over this, you know as well as I do that they will agree that I must carry out the wishes expressed in your sister's will."

"I think not," the Marquis said slowly, almost drawling the words. "I have asked my Solicitors to discover when the will was made and I am informed that it was signed by my sister and witnessed four days before she died."

He paused and. as Lord Burnham did not speak. He then went on,

"A number of my relatives visited her during that last week, who will confirm that she was semiconscious and completely incapable of conversing with them."

"That is untrue!" Lord Burnham shouted.

"They would be prepared to say that on oath and the doctors and nurses who attended my sister would also be called upon to give their evidence."

Listening and watching Lord Burnham, Athina realised how very astute the Marquis was being.

The older man seemed to shrink and there was no bluster left in him.

Instead he said in a surly manner,

"That child has cost me a great deal of money."

"Which, of course. will be reimbursed to you," the Marquis said, "but I intend to ask that my sister's fortune be held in Trust for the boy. We will then work out an arrangement without your having the administration of it solely in your hands, as you have had until now."

Lord Burnham clenched his fists..

For a heart-pounding moment Athina thought that he was going to strike the Marquis.

Then he exclaimed furiously,

"*Curse you*! May you rot in hell and the boy with you!"

As he spoke furiously and ferociously, Lord Burnham walked past the Marquis and reached the door.

He pulled it open and then turned back.

"I will get even with you, Denzil, sooner or later!" he snarled.

He went out into the corridor, slamming the door behind him.

Athina put her hands up to her face.

The tension had been intolerable and even now she could hardly believe that they had won.

The Marquis raised himself from the arm of the chair.

"It might have been worse," he remarked coolly.

Then he looked at Athina.

"You are all right?"

"I feel as if I have just been battered by a tornado, but you were wonderful! I am sure he now realises that he can never have Peter back."

"I do hope so," the Marquis murmured quietly.

"How could you have guessed so cleverly that he had written the will himself when your sister was dying? And I suppose he guided her hand so that she could sign it."

"I have always thought it strange," the Marquis said, "that Louise should have left her son, whom she adored, to be looked after by his stepfather rather than any of our female relatives, who I know would have been only too willing to have him."

"Yet – you did – nothing about it."

"There appeared to be no reason why I should," the Marquis said a little guiltily. "I knew that Burnham was a somewhat aggressive chap, but it is only lately that he has taken to drinking so heavily and I have the uncomfortable suspicion that it was because he could now afford it on Peter's money."

"Can you really take it back for Peter?"

"That is what I fully intend to do," the Marquis answered in a voice of determination.

Athina rose from the sofa.

"Let's go and tell Peter that he need no longer be afraid and this is his home from now on."

She walked towards the door and the Marquis joined her.

"That is one problem solved, but you must not forget mine."

Athina smiled.

"Have you let the Queen know that you are now engaged, my Lord?"

"I have written a letter to the Lord Chamberlain," the Marquis replied, "but, of course, these things take time and it would seem very strange if, immediately after my appointment, you then threw me out as unwanted."

Athina laughed.

"I will not do that until you tell me it is impossible for the Queen to take back what she had already given you."

"Thank you on my behalf," the Marquis said, "but I think Peter would be very upset if you left here."

"Mrs. Beckwith and I are very comfortable at Rock Park," Athina responded demurely.

"I really don't know whether it is me or Mrs. Field who should be gratified by that remark!" the Marquis retorted.

They were both laughing as they hurried up to the sitting room that had been allotted to Peter as his schoolroom.

They knew that he would be waiting, trembling and apprehensive, until they reached him.

*

The next day Athina felt as if the dark clouds had vanished from the sky.

Peter was in high spirits as they rode with the Marquis over the estate and he showed them some of the improvements he was making.

It surprised him how much Athina knew about farming methods.

He learned that she not only had, as she had told him, a number of breeding mares at Murling Park but also a pig farm, which was doing exceptionally well.

"That is something I had not thought of," he admitted. "You must take me over and show me your estate. It is not very far to go."

"Not if we ride," Athina agreed. "But it takes far longer if we go by road."

"Then we will ride," the Marquis said firmly.

"Please, may I come too?" Peter implored him. "I would love to see Aunt Athina's horses and find out if they are as good as yours."

"They are not," Athina said, "but I love them just as they are."

She spoke a little defiantly and the Marquis was about to answer when Peter intervened,

"I worry about poor Ladybird. Do you think that Step-Papa is still beating her? Her back was all sores like mine."

"I will tell you what I will do," the Marquis stated. "If indeed your stepfather is hard up, as I think he is, I will, if it is at all possible, buy Ladybird from him. She will be your special horse."

"Oh – could you – would you really?" Peter enthused. "She is such a – lovely mare and I don't – think that anybody was – kind to her – except for me.

"I promise I will try," the Marquis replied. "Then you can make her happy at Rock Park with you."

"I am happy, very very happy! It's only when I think about Ladybird that I am sad."

"Leave it to me," the Marquis smiled.

Athina felt that no one could be kinder or more understanding of the feelings of a small boy.

Now, as they toured round the estate, the Marquis explained to her why he had stayed away from Rock Park for so long.

Her father had been wrong in believing that he had only wanted to enjoy himself in London. He was feeling what any young man would, frustrated and offended, because nobody would listen to him.

His father would not consider even for a single moment the many improvements to the estate that he knew were very necessary.

"We will go over to Murling Park first thing tomorrow morning," the Marquis proposed now.

"We will have luncheon there," Athina answered, "and perhaps you could send a groom to warn my servants to prepare a good meal."

She paused before she added,

"Mrs. Bell has been the cook ever since I was a small child and, of course, although her food cannot rival that of your chef, I hope you will find it eatable."

"I am sure I shall," the Marquis declared, "and I shall be very interested to see your home."

Athina thought that it would be rather fun to show it to him.

It would not in any way compare with the magnificence of Rock Park.

It was a very old house and very picturesque and she thought that the Marquis might find it interesting to compare the two estates.

She was beginning to feel guilty that in staying at Rock Park she was neglecting her duties at home.

At the same time she knew that it would greatly upset Peter if she left him.

The Marquis was quite right in thinking that not for a moment did anyone question that their engagement was anything but genuine.

She thought it highly amusing to be deceiving the Queen of all people.

Her Majesty had been really unfair in insisting that the Marquis should be married or engaged before he would be able to take up the post of the Master of the Horse.

"What are you thinking about?" the Marquis asked unexpectedly.

"I was actually thinking that you will make a very good Master of the Horse and, since your uncle, Lord Edward Rock, was not really a good horseman, I am sure that there will be a great deal to be done to the Royal Stables."

"That is what I thought," the Marquis agreed with satisfaction, "and I intend to make the Queen's Stud outstanding."

Athina was feeling certain that, as in everything else she could mention, he would succeed in his aims.

She realised that he was in many ways an exceptional man.

"I shall be very grateful for your advice about Murling Park," she said aloud. "I have put in many innovations since I have been running it, but when I saw yours I recognised how much more there is for me to do."

"I hope you will let me help you," the Marquis replied simply.

"I should be very disappointed if you did not," Athina replied.

Peter went off sleepily to bed after an early supper.

At dinner that night the Marquis had insisted that Athina and Mrs. Beckwith celebrate with him the victory that had been won over Lord Burnham.

They drank champagne and, as they sipped it, Athina asked him,

"You are quite certain he has not a trump card up his sleeve? Will he do something we have not thought of that will upset Peter?"

"I doubt it. I have already written to my Solicitors to tell them that he is to receive a considerable sum of money every year so long as he does not dispute my Guardianship and does not interfere with Peter in any way."

"That is marvellous!" Athina cried.

"He needs the money," the Marquis said in a satisfied tone, "and, if he troubles us in the future, we will simply stop the payments."

Athina looked at him with admiration in her eyes. He thought it was certainly an improvement on the way that she had looked at him when they had first met.

*

The next morning Peter was in a state of excitement at the idea of going to Murling Park.

"You must show me all your horses, Aunt Athina," he urged, "and I expect they will be thrilled to see you."

"I am sure they will," Athina agreed. "And the names that I have given them are Greek just like my own. You must tell them to Mrs. Beckwith who will certainly have a story about each of the Gods and Goddesses who they have been named after."

"Mrs. Beckwith's stories are jolly good," Peter praised her. "She plays a game with me when we do arithmetic, which makes it fun!"

Athina knew from her own experience what a clever Teacher Mrs. Beckwith was. She thought, as she had thought before, how fortunate Peter was to have her to teach him

The one thing that she could not teach him was riding.

"You are quite certain you don't want to come with us?" Athina asked her.

Mrs. Beckwith shook her head.

"I will come with you another day when we go in the chaise or in his Lordship's dog cart," she replied.

"And I will come with you too," Peter said. "I want to see the dogs running underneath it."

He had already made friends with the Marquis's Dalmatians and Athina was looking forward to showing him her spaniels.

She wondered if she could ask the Marquis if she could bring one back with her. But she was concerned that he might object to adding to the dogs that were already running loose about the house.

The horses were waiting in the drive for them after breakfast.

Just as they went outside to mount them, Dawson came to tell the Marquis that one of the farmers wanted to see him.

"There's been a spot of bother at his farm, my Lord," he related. "The roof has fallen in."

"I had better come to see him at once," the Marquis answered.

By now Athina and Peter were already mounted.

"You two go on ahead," the Marquis suggested, "and I will catch up with you. I should not be very long."

"We will not hurry, my Lord," Athina replied. "I expect you know the way. It is through Monk's Wood."

"I will find you quite easily," the Marquis confirmed.

He then went back into the house.

Athina and Peter rode out of the courtyard and down the drive towards the lake.

They crossed over the ancient bridge that spanned it and then they rode under the trees in the Park.

They disturbed the deer and they moved away from them, but not very fast because they were almost tame.

At the far end of the Park they could now see Monk's Wood.

There was a ride cut through it that led eventually to the Murling Estate.

Athina remembered that when she was a small girl there had been at one time an extremely heated argument between her father and the late Marquis.

The Earl had complained to the Marquis that his guests who shot close by Monk's Wood were killing his pheasants.

The Marquis on the other hand, asserted that when the Earl shot near to that particular boundary it was the Rock Park pheasants that were being killed. It was an argument that had no ending and had droned on for years.

It was now a delightfully warm sunny day and the woods looked very beautiful and the leaves of the trees were still the pale green of spring.

The bluebells were over, but there were still some wild daffodils left to give a touch of gold to the hedgerows and peeping from among their leaves were purple and white violets.

The path narrowed and Athina led the way with Peter following behind her.

There was still no sign of the Marquis and she therefore rode more slowly.

She so wanted to see the expression on his face when he first saw Murling Park.

It was a low-built house with diamond-paned windows and it had the strange, thick, twisting chimneys of the Elizabethan era.

Everyone, when they first saw the house, exclaimed immediately at how romantic it looked and she wondered to herself what adjective the Marquis would use.

They reached the centre of the wood and here the ride was a little wider and Athina pulled in her horse.

"I wonder what is keeping your uncle?" she asked.

"He will soon catch up with us if he rides very fast," Peter replied.

"I cannot hear him coming," Athina pointed out a little anxiously.

Then, as she glanced round, she called out,

"Look, Peter! There is a poor little bird that must have just fallen out of its nest or been thrown out by a cuckoo."

Peter bent forward to look to where Athina was pointing.

There, sure enough, were two little baby birds lying on the ground with their beaks open.

He bent down further so that he could take a closer look.

It saved his life.

There was an explosion of gunfire and a bullet buried itself in the tree in front of him.

Athina gave a gasp and Peter exclaimed,

"What was – that?"

"Ride! Ride quickly! Go, go!" she shouted at him.

Obediently he passed her.

She pulled her horse in behind him to shelter him from any further danger.

Peter then rode off at a tremendous pace through the wood and Athina just managed to keep up with him.

As they came to the end of the trees and rode on out into an open field, Peter reined in his horse.

"Somebody – shot at – me – Aunt Athina!" he exclaimed.

Before Athina could answer him, she saw the Marquis to her very considerable relief.

He must have passed through the wood a little higher up and he was now coming down the field at a sharp canter.

"Tell your uncle what happened," she said.

Peter obediently rode towards him.

As he did so, Athina surmised that they had been too optimistic in believing that they had won the battle.

Lord Burnham, as she had thought from the very first, would be a relentless enemy.

CHAPTER SIX

Peter galloped up to the Marquis.

"Someone shot at me, Uncle Denzil," he yelled, "the bullet went straight past – my head!"

The Marquis stared at him and then he said,

"Come on, let's get away from here."

He started to ride across the field in the direction of the Murling Estate.

Seeing what they were doing, Athina followed them.

They went across another field and only as they reached the trees that bordered the drive of her house did the Marquis pull in his horse.

"I will tell you what happened," Athina said as she joined them. "We were riding through the wood slowly as we were waiting for you to catch up with us. Then we stopped to hear if you were coming and I saw a bird that had fallen out of its nest."

"There were two, there were two," Peter interposed.

"There were two," Athina corrected herself. "Peter bent forward to look at them and as he did so – a shot rang out and the bullet buried itself in a tree, passing just where Peter's head would – have been."

She saw the Marquis's lips tighten.

As her voice faltered, he realised that she was very pale and it had obviously been a tremendous shock for her.

He put out his hand.

Athina had already taken off her glove to press her hand to her face and instead she put it into his.

She felt that the strength of his fingers was very comforting.

"Are you all right?" he asked her.

"Yes," she answered. "I-I am all – right."

She did not sound very certain about it and the Marquis looked at her searchingly as he said,

"Let's go on to your house. I don't imagine that there is anything we can do at present. The man who fired a shot at Peter will have made a quick getaway by now."

As he spoke, Athina saw her gamekeeper coming down the drive with two dogs at his heels.

She took her hand from the Marquis's and told him,

"There is Wilkins, my gamekeeper."

The Marquis rode up to the man and, as he touched his forelock, said to him,

"There is, we think, a poacher in Monk's Wood. As I cannot get hold of any of my keepers in a hurry, I would be grateful if you would go and see what is happening. Her Ladyship heard a shot as she was coming here."

"I'll go at once, my Lord," Wilkins answered. "Them poachers be everywhere and they does a lot of damage to the young birds!"

"I know that only too well," the Marquis replied.

The gamekeeper walked away and his dogs followed him.

When he was out of earshot, the Marquis said,

"I doubt if he will find anybody there. They would not stay to be caught."

"Do you think that it was Step-Papa who was trying to – kill me?" Peter asked him nervously.

"It was probably just a poacher, as I said to the gamekeeper," the Marquis replied, "shooting the pigeons."

He spoke casually, but Athina was well aware that he was trying to prevent Peter from being frightened.

She knew that she herself was terrified.

Just how was it possible in the quiet of the country that someone could be lurking on the Marquis's land waiting to murder Peter?

It could be Lord Burnham himself.

But more likely it was someone he had hired to do his dirty work for him.

'What are we – to do? *What – are we to – do*?' she asked herself, as they rode on up the drive.

The Marquis was looking at Murling Park with great interest and, as they neared it, he said,

"I had completely forgotten, for I have not been here since I was about twelve, how beautiful your house is."

"I hoped you would think so," Athina answered.

"There is nothing more attractive," the Marquis went on, "than the pink of all those Elizabethan bricks when they have been mellowed by the centuries."

Athina managed to smile. He was right and he was appreciating her home.

There were two grooms waiting to take their horses and, as they walked up to the front door, an ancient butler opened it.

Next there was the patter of feet as three small spaniels then came bursting out.

They all jumped up at Athina barking excitedly because she had come home.

As she bent to pat them, Peter did the same.

"They are very pleased to see you, Aunt Athina," he shouted above the noise that the dogs were making.

Athina was making a particular fuss of one outstandingly good-looking spaniel.

"This is Flash," she said to Peter. "I have had him ever since he was born. He goes everywhere with me when I am at home."

"He must have missed you while you were at Rock Park," Peter remarked.

"You can see he did," Athina replied.

Flash was trying in every way he knew to tell her how glad he was that she was back at home.

The Marquis was watching.

As she gave the spaniel a final pat and rose to her feet, he said,

"I can see I have been very remiss in not including Flash among my guests."

Athina's eyes lit up.

"Do you really mean that I can bring him to Rock Park? I had thought of asking you, but I was afraid it would be an imposition."

Before the Marquis could reply Peter chimed in,

"Oh, please, Uncle Denzil, do let Aunt Athina bring Flash to stay with us. I will look after him and he can sleep in my room."

Athina thought that this was an excellent idea and Flash would certainly help to protect him.

If by any chance an intruder entered Peter's bedroom, she knew that Flash would bark loudly and very likely attack him.

There was no need to express in words what she was thinking.

As she glanced at the Marquis, she was aware that he thought the same as her.

"We will take Flash back with us to Rock Park," he affirmed.

Athina then took him over the house.

She felt touched that he greatly appreciated the low ceilings, the diamond-paned windows and the huge open fireplaces. It was all so very different from his own house.

Peter was delighted with everything he saw.

When they finally sat down in the dining room for luncheon, she thought with much satisfaction that Mrs. Bell had excelled herself.

She had cooked several delicious dishes that they all enjoyed to the full.

When luncheon was over, they went into the garden and Peter started throwing a ball for Flash and the other dogs.

Athina and the Marquis sat down on a wooden seat in the Rose Garden.

It was the first time they had been alone together without Peter and Athina asked the Marquis tentatively,

"What are you going to do about – the man in the wood, my Lord?"

"There is really nothing that I can do," the Marquis answered. "I am certain that your gamekeeper will find nothing by the time he gets there."

"But – he will – try again," Athina faltered.

"I am aware of that," the Marquis said, "but I can hardly confine Peter to the house or send him out only under armed guard."

Athina made a helpless little gesture with her hands.

"I am – frightened, very – *very* – frightened."

"I can easily understand and so we can only pray that we will be protected."

She was so surprised at what he had just said that she looked at him questioningly.

"If you think about it," he said quietly, "Fate, or Peter's Guardian Angel, brought you into his life at the very moment when, if I am not mistaken, Burnham was intent on murdering him."

"How can it be possible that a man, who is in the House of Lords and has held high Government posts, be actually prepared to commit murder?" Athina asked.

"Then his financial position must be even worse than I thought," the Marquis replied. "I am convinced now that he married my sister entirely for her money, even though he was in fact genuinely attracted by her."

Athina made no comment and the Marquis went on as if he was puzzling it all out for himself,

"I was very surprised when she married again. She was broken-hearted at the sudden death of Gerald Naver. He was a charming and delightful person whom everybody loved."

"Then why did she marry so soon after he died?" Athina asked.

"I suppose the truth was that she did not care what happened to her," the Marquis replied, "and when Burnham wooed her so ardently, she thought it would be good for Peter to have another father."

"I can well understand it," Athina murmured slowly.

"As we now know, it was disastrous," the Marquis went on, "and, when Burnham knew that Louise was dying, he was determined to get all the money for himself."

"Which is – what he – wants now."

"As I have told you, I have already arranged for him to be offered a very considerable annual income," the Marquis said, "but I gather now from what happened this afternoon that it is not enough for him."

There was a distinct note of anger in his voice as he spoke and Athina looked at the squareness of his chin and the expression in his eyes.

She thought that he was like a Knight going into battle against the Powers of Darkness.

Then she ruminated that it was a strange way to be thinking of the Marquis whom at first she had so strongly disliked and disapproved of.

Yet how could she disapprove of him now when he was fighting so determinedly for Peter's life.

Peter then came running back to them and panted,

"Flash is quicker than all the other dogs! He always gets the ball first."

"That is why I called him *Flash*," Athina answered. "Even as a puppy he was very quick-witted and gobbled up his dinner far quicker than the rest."

Peter laughed.

"That is what Uncle Denzil likes me to do. I am getting fat. My riding breeches already are getting too tight round my tummy."

"You must tell Mrs. Field," Athina said. "I feel sure that she will have another pair a little bigger that once belonged to your uncle."

"I will tell her," Peter said, "but I think in about a week I will want a bigger pair still!"

They laughed and Peter ran off again to play with the dogs.

Athina suddenly felt afraid that within a week or so he might not be there.

She turned to the Marquis.

"What can – we do? Or rather – what can – *you* do?" she asked.

"That is what I am trying to puzzle out," he replied, "and I think now we should return to Rock Park. We will go by a roundabout way that will take much longer than going through Monk's Wood."

Athina shivered.

She could still hear in her mind the sound of the shot as the bullet buried itself in the tree behind Peter.

She did not speak, but the Marquis knew what she was thinking.

"Trust me," he urged her. "At the same time Peter must never be left alone."

"No, of course not," Athina agreed at once.

The horses were brought round to the front door and Athina said 'goodbye' to Mrs. Bell and thanked her for the splendid luncheon.

She then told Upton, the old butler, to look after everything.

"Will your ladyship be a-coming back soon?" he asked.

"I am not sure, Upton, but I know that everything will be safe in your capable hands and his Lordship may wish to come over again in a day or so."

Because of what had happened in the wood, they had not gone to see her mares or the pigs as she had intended.

She sensed that the Marquis felt the same as she did.

If they were to stray too far from the house, it would be easy for a gunman to take another shot at Peter.

They mounted their horses.

The. Marquis moved off quickly leading them through the stables instead of down the drive.

He rode away from the house in a different direction from the one that he would have taken if they were returning straight to Rock Park and Peter was happy riding behind his uncle on a well-bred horse.

He did not therefore seem to notice that they were returning to Rock Park by a different route.

He chattered on about the birds, the sheep and the cattle that they passing and he kept an eye on Flash who was running behind them.

It was not until they came in sight of Rock Park that he said,

"That was a really long way to go home, Uncle Denzil. But it was a scrumptious ride!"

"I am glad you enjoyed it," the Marquis said, "and I think we will ride straight into the stables instead of dismounting at the front door as we usually do."

Peter made no comment.

Athina knew that the Marquis was avoiding the open courtyard at the front of the house. If anyone was watching for them, it was where he would expect them to dismount.

They rode into the stables where several grooms and stable lads were moving about.

Athina was not surprised when the Marquis then took them into the house by the kitchen door.

He made the excuse that he wanted to show Peter the dairy. There were huge bowls of milk left on marble slabs every night so that there would be plenty of cream in the morning.

Peter was fascinated by it, but Athina, however, well knew that the servants were surprised to see the Marquis in an area of Rock Park that he did not usually visit.

They reached the hall and the main staircase.

Peter ran up it, calling Flash so that he could show the dog to Mrs. Beckwith.

She was sitting very comfortably in an armchair and, as Athina had expected, reading a book.

As Peter rushed in, he told her first about Flash and how he had come to stay with them.

Then he remembered to tell her that a shot had been fired at him.

When he did so, he said,

"It was very – frightening, but Aunt Athina told me to ride away quickly and so I galloped out of the wood as fast as I could go. Then I saw – Uncle Denzil."

"It all sounds horrifying to me," Mrs. Beckwith exclaimed, "but lots of Kings and Queens have been shot at. Tomorrow we will find some books about them and you will see that they were as brave as you were."

"That will be fun," Peter smiled.

He then ran down the corridor to his bedroom to change from his riding breeches.

Mrs. Beckwith turned to Athina,

"How can this happen in England of all places? And here in the country where everything is always so peaceful."

"That is what I have been asking," Athina replied, "and, if it had not been for the baby birds, Peter would now be dead!"

Mrs. Beckwith put a hand on her arm.

"I am certain that the Marquis will do something about that man," she maintained. "This cannot go on!"

"That is exactly what I have been saying," Athina answered, "but how can we know when he will strike again?"

She felt the tears come into her eyes and hurried to her own room to change.

She came downstairs for tea in the drawing room and Athina by this time felt more composed and she knew that it would be a mistake to keep talking about what had happened.

Instead, when Mrs. Beckwith joined them, they then talked about Murling Park and its fascination.

"It is reputed that Queen Elizabeth once slept in the house on one of her journeys across the country," Athina remarked.

"The number of houses supposed to have put her up for the night are so many," the Marquis joined in sarcastically. "So I can only think that Her Majesty never stopped travelling around her Kingdom and so found London itself very boring."

"That is the opposite of what you thought," Athina said teasingly. "When I first heard about you from my father, he told that me that he had no use for the young 'toffs' who only wanted to enjoy themselves with beautiful women in London and were bored in the country."

The Marquis laughed.

"Was that really my reputation?"

"It was much worse than that," Athina went on, "but I am far too polite to mention it!"

The Marquis was about to expostulate when Peter said,

"I love being in the country. I want just to live here and ride Uncle Denzil's horses. And I want dozens and dozens of dogs like Flash."

"Not all in the house, I would hope!" the Marquis said quickly. "My carpets are very valuable."

"I would train them so well that they never did anything naughty," Peter promised.

"That would surely be a step in the right direction," the Marquis admitted.

Flash was content to play with Peter and they scrambled about on the floor together.

Watching them, Athina thought that it was difficult to recognise the pale, frightened, half-starved little boy sobbing so miserably for his mother when she had first met him.

When later on they sat talking in the drawing room, she felt that anyone who saw them would think that they were just an ordinary family with no great problems to solve.

Certainly not with a murderer worrying them.

'Lord Burnham should be hanged!' she said to herself.

She shied away from the thought that she and the Marquis might be worrying over their own son.

Whether their conversation would be taking place in a cottage or in the magnificence of Rock Park, it would be just the same.

'The sooner Lord Burnham is out of our lives and I can go home, the better,' she decided.

Because she was always honest with herself, she knew that for the moment at any rate she would rather be at Rock Park alone with the Marquis.

Peter then asked that he might have dinner with them.

The Marquis agreed, mainly Athina thought, because he would then be able to keep his eye on him.

While the boy was with them, nobody had to worry about what was happening to him.

As Athina put on one of her pretty gowns she had bought to wear in London, she thought how extraordinary the Marquis was.

He usually had his friends staying with him at Rock Park, she supposed.

Now he was apparently very content to have just herself and Mrs. Beckwith.

Actually she herself should be staying in London at this moment preparing to be presented to Queen Victoria at Buckingham Palace. And she would be counting her many invitations to the balls as they arrived every morning.

She had written a letter that was almost truthful to the relation she had arranged to stay with.

She had explained that she had encountered very many problems at Murling Park and so could not leave.

She added,

"It may be a question of a week or perhaps only days and by now you may have seen the announcement in The London Gazette that I am engaged to the Marquis of Rockingdale.

I know that Papa would be so pleased as our estates march with each other. As soon as I can come to London, you will meet him and I am sure you will find him delightful – "

She then wrote more or less the same letter to her other relatives, making the same excuse for not coming to London immediately.

She was certain that they would think it extraordinary when her coming out had all been arranged.

Then she reflected,

'They will surely expect me to attend the first drawing room at Buckingham Palace and then another one after I am married.'

Yet it was impossible for her to leave Peter just now.

Besides if she and the Marquis took Peter to London with them, it would be easier for him to have an unfortunate 'accident' of some sort there.

After dinner, when Mrs. Beckwith had taken Peter upstairs to bed, Athina and the Marquis were left alone.

It was then that she admitted,

"I am feeling very guilty. I am sure you ought to be in London enjoying the Season, just as I should be, my Lord. And yet I am afraid of going there with Peter in case it is even more dangerous than here."

"It is dangerous wherever he goes," the Marquis said, "but once I catch Burnham red-handed, I can threaten him so that he will be too frightened to try again."

"How could you do that?" Athina asked.

"He is afraid of a scandal and I would, of course, accuse him of attempted murder."

Athina gave a little cry.

"Can – you really do – so?"

"If I catch him in the act," the Marquis said. "Alternatively I can force him to live abroad and give him enough money to stay there."

"That would be a far better solution," Athina said, "Oh, please – please – let's hope that – we don't have to – wait too long."

"Are you already so bored already with being here with me?" the Marquis asked unexpectedly.

"No, of course not," Athina replied rapidly, "but I feel very guilty when I think of how boring it must be for you."

"I have not said I am bored," the Marquis assured her. "In fact, although I agree with you that the situation is frightening, I have never felt more alert and more purposeful. I am determined to rid us of this menace, which is certainly very bad for Peter as well as for you."

"I do not – matter, but he is such a – dear little boy and – one day he will – have to go to school."

"I can only hope to God that I shall have dealt with Burnham long before that," the Marquis said sharply.

Athina then thought that it had been a tactless thing for her to say.

It implied that the Marquis would seriously have to continue with his protection of Peter rather than live his own life.

She then wondered about how many lovely ladies were finding it extraordinary that he continued to stay in the country where they could not see him.

She thought how dull it must be for him to have only her and Mrs. Beckwith to talk to. In London there had been the dazzling beauties who frequented Marlborough House.

"If we are talking about people missing London," the Marquis suggested, "what about you? I understand from Mrs. Beckwith that you expected to be presented to the Queen at the first drawing room and should by now be counting your invitations to balls."

It was something Athina had herself been thinking of in identical words and she answered swiftly,

"Nothing matters. Nothing and nobody except Peter! Anyway, as I am a country girl, I prefer being here to staying in London."

"That is just nonsense!" the Marquis said argumentatively. "You know perfectly well that it is the dream of every young woman to be the belle of the ball, the beauty of the Season and have a dozen young men asking for her hand in marriage."

Athina laughed.

"I think it more likely that I shall be joining the endless rows of *debutantes* whom, I am told, smart gentlemen like yourself ignore as if they had the plague!"

The Marquis chuckled.

"I must admit that I don't know any *debutantes* nor have I ever even spoken to one! But they do exist and I suppose they have their place in the Social world."

"Most men have to marry some time," Athina said, "and one day when all this is over you will inevitably find yourself walking down the aisle with a ravishing *debutante* who is the beauty of the Season."

"That is exactly what I have always been afraid of," the Marquis replied, "and I suppose it is what will happen to me if the Queen has her way."

He spoke aggressively and there was silence until Athina asked,

"When we break off our engagement, you don't think that your position as the Master of the Horse will be taken away from you?"

"It is what the Queen might want to do," the Marquis replied in a serious tone. "At the same time, if I prove myself, as I intend to be, really good at my job, it will be difficult for her to find a plausible excuse for dismissing me."

"I am glad about that, my Lord."

"And of course while we are talking about it," the Marquis said, "if the man of your dreams comes down the chimney or you meet him unexpectedly, then you must tell me immediately and we will put the wheels in motion to set you free."

"Meanwhile you are quite safe," Athina commented. "Unless you have invited a number of your friends to stay, I am not likely to meet any eligible bachelors."

"Is that what you want?" the Marquis enquired.

"You know it is not!" Athina replied. "I have already told you that I have no wish to be married and I would never marry anyone unless I was very much – in love."

"And how will you know if that is what you are feeling?"

She looked at him in a rather startled fashion.

"I have never thought of it," she replied, "but I suppose one does know when one is in love. One must feel different or is that just a lot of nonsense invented by the poets?"

The Marquis smiled.

"I do promise you, Athina, that, when you are in love, you will be very much aware of it."

There was silence for a moment.

Then she asked him,

"Is it a very – very – wonderful feeling?"

"So I have always been told," the Marquis answered.

She looked at him in astonishment.

"You have always been *told?*" she repeated. "But surely you must have been in love – dozens of times?"

The Marquis seemed for the moment to be at a loss for words.

Then he said,

"Real love, which is what you have in mind, is what the poets write about and it is not the same as what passes for love in the Social world. It is something very different."

"How is that – possible?" Athina asked him with a puzzled look on her face.

"Men and women have been physically attracted to each other since the beginning of creation," the Marquis told her, "which is right and natural."

He paused as if he was choosing his words before he went on,

"But such attraction is something very different from what we are talking about and which you are very ignorant of at the moment."

"How is it different?" Athina asked impulsively.

She was enthralled by this conversation and it was something that she had never talked about with anyone before.

Her father had once told her when she had asked him,

"When I was very young, I fell very much in love with a beautiful girl but she married somebody else."

"Were you very unhappy, Papa?" Athina had asked.

"Because I was young and impetuous," her father replied, "I felt suicidal. But eventually there were other women about, who, although I never did feel the same again for any one of them, made me almost forget what I had suffered."

It was unlike her father to be so communicative about his past, but after that he had never referred to the subject again.

She had often wondered if that was why he had never really got on with her mother.

Her mother too had been in love and she had said that her heart had been totally broken when she could not marry the man she called 'William'.

The Marquis was looking at Athina while she was thinking and after a moment he said,

"You are certainly very lovely, Athina, and altogether worthy of your Greek Goddess name. I can promise you that when you do get to London there will be many men who will lay their hearts at your feet!"

"But – supposing," Athina asked in a small voice, "my heart does not – respond?"

"If you are wise," the Marquis advised, "you will stick to your guns and refuse to marry until the right man finally comes along."

"That is what I want to do," Athina murmured quietly.

"Let me assure you that he will come along," the Marquis said, "and then you will instinctively know what real love is and that it is exactly what you have dreamt about."

Athina thought that this really told her very little about what she really wanted to know.

They then talked of other things and laughed a great deal. Yet she was still thinking of love when she walked slowly upstairs to bed.

She went into Peter's room and saw that he was fast asleep. The Marquis had arranged that Peter slept in the room next to hers.

Mrs. Beckwith was some distance away and next to the delightful room that the Marquis had allotted to Peter as his schoolroom.

His Master suite was just a little further along down the corridor.

Athina was aware that, if things had been normal, he would have been put on the nurseries floor.

As she went to her own room, she thought it would be impossible for anyone to get at him from outside the house.

When she had looked into Peter's room, she had seen Flash curled up at the bottom of his bed.

He did not jump up and go to her as he usually did. Instead he just wagged his tail.

She knew that with the instinct of an intelligent dog he understood that he was there to guard Peter.

She patted him gently and looked at Peter as he slept.

She then went from the room, carrying the candle that she had lit on her way upstairs.

The Marquis had installed electric light in most of the bedrooms.

But, because it was traditional, every guest was handed a candle by a footman before they went upstairs to bed.

It was something that had always been done at Murling Park too and her father had insisted on it.

Athina recognised that she would greatly miss the candles if they were superseded by modern appliances.

In her own room she put the candle down by her bed and left it burning. There was no doubt in this magnificent State room with its four-poster bed that candlelight was far more romantic.

There was a small candelabrum holding three lit candles on her dressing table so she ignored the new light-switch beside the door and undressed by candlelight.

She had told the maid that she would not need her.

She was thinking now of the strange conversation that she had had with the Marquis about love. Never had she expected him to speak out like that or to admit what he was looking for.

It was not what was accepted by the 'Smart Set' who were centred round the Prince of Wales.

'Supposing I never find love?' Athina asked as she had put on her nightgown.

Then she told herself that there was so much beauty and romance in the world and she could not be the only person to be left out.

She longed to find the love that was very beautiful, very desirable and very inspiring.

She went to the window to pull back the curtains.

There was a cloud over the moon and so the lake was not turned to silver as it had been on other nights and the Park was dark and so seemed somewhat forbidding.

Unable to find in it the message that she was seeking, she pulled the curtains to again.

Blowing out the three candles on her dressing table, she climbed into bed.

She lay there wondering whether she should pray that one day she would find love. It was something that she had never done before.

Yet now, as she thought about what the Marquis had said to her, she had the strange feeling that it was love that he too was praying he would find.

Not on his knees and not in actual words, but in his heart.

Although it seemed to her most surprising that love had eluded him.

'He is indeed a very strange man,' she told herself, 'and so utterly different from what I might have expected.'

CHAPTER SEVEN

Athina did not fall asleep at once.

She was going over in her mind everything that had happened day by day.

She felt as if they were all standing on the edge of a precipice.

Just one puff of wind would send them hurtling down into some dreadful depths that they would never be able to escape from.

'What shall – we do? *What can – we do?*'

The very walls were repeating the words in her mind.

Then at last she fell asleep.

She was then dreaming that she was galloping with the Marquis over a field that had no end.

They galloped and galloped side by side.

Then she heard a little voice say,

"Aunt – Athina! I – want – you!"

Peter was standing by her bed,

He had left the door open and the light coming from the sconces in the corridor silhouetted his head.

"Peter!" Athina exclaimed, "What is the matter?"

"I was – dreaming – of Mum-ma," Peter said in a hesitating voice, "and she – told me to get up. I got up – Aunt Athina – and when I – then looked out of the window – I saw Step-Papa –I am sure it – was him – riding up the drive on a horse."

Knowing how dark it was outside now, Athina thought that this was most unlikely and part of his dream and he really could have seen nothing.

Yet she could tell that he was feeling genuinely frightened.

"Climb into bed with me and you can tell me what your mother said and if you could see her clearly. It must have been very exciting for you."

Peter scrambled onto the bed and slipped between the sheets.

"Now – I feel – safe," he muttered.

"You are safe here," Athina assured him, "and no one will harm you."

She drew him close to her and kissed him.

As she did so, she realised that he was still half-asleep.

"Close your eyes," she said softly, "and think about your Mama. I am sure she is near you – and is protecting you."

Peter then snuggled down against the pillows and Athina got out of bed.

By the light coming through the door she could see her *negligée* on a chair.

She put it on and then went to the window to discover if it was in fact possible that he could have seen Lord Burnham coming up the drive.

She pulled the curtain a little way to one side and looked out.

It was very dark with the moon still hidden behind a thick bank of cloud and the stars were barely reflected in the lake.

As far as she could see the drive with its oak trees was empty.

She could only just make out the outline of the ancient bridge that spanned the lake.

Her eyes travelled from the bridge to a thick cluster of shrubs and they hid from view the stable buildings at one side of the house.

She stared at them intently and her eyes were now growing more accustomed to the darkness.

She thought, although it might have been part of her imagination, that she saw a movement in the shrubs.

She could not be certain, although she leaned out of the window trying to see more clearly.

There was not a breath of wind and everything was absolutely still.

Then she thought, although she still could not be sure, that there really was some movement among the shrubs.

She felt fear streak through her as if it was lightning.

Turning from the window she moved across the room towards the bed.

Peter was breathing rhythmically and there was no doubt that he was fast asleep.

She looked at him for a moment.

Then she went out into the corridor, closing the door behind her.

She ran the short distance to the Marquis's suit.

The outer door opened into a small hall and she could see that there was another door into the bedroom itself.

She did not knock, she just walked in.

As she did so, she realised that the room was not in darkness as there was a light by the bed.

A huge four-poster bed hung with red velvet had the family Coat of Arms embroidered above the headboard.

The Marquis was lying in the bed propped up on several pillows.

He had obviously been reading a book that lay open in front of him and while reading it he had obviously fallen asleep.

His eyes were closed and his head was against the pillows behind him.

Frightened though she was feeling, Athina was well aware that he looked exceedingly handsome.

Just for a moment she hesitated as to whether she ought to wake him up.

Then she remembered that Peter said he had been woken by his mother and she knew that wherever she might be, Lady Louise was trying to protect her son.

Athina moved closer and touched the Marquis's hand, which lay on the book.

"Wake up, my Lord," she said urgently. "*Wake up!*"

The Marquis, having once been a soldier, was instantly alert.

"Athina!" he exclaimed. "What is it?"

"I think, but it may be just – my imagination," Athina explained, "that there is – somebody moving about – in the shrubs at the side of the courtyard."

The Marquis did not stop to argue with her, he quickly jumped out of bed.

Going to a chair where his valet had left his long dark robe, he put it on.

"Is Peter asleep?" he asked.

"He came to me," Athina answered, "saying that he had dreamt of his mother who had told him to get up. When he then looked out of the window, he thought he saw his stepfather riding up the drive."

She saw the surprise on the Marquis's face and added quickly,

"He was half-asleep and it is so dark that I did not think he could really have seen anything – but I do think that something or someone is – moving about in the – shrubs."

As she spoke, she was afraid that the Marquis would think that she was just being hysterical.

The movement, if she had seen it, had been very slight.

At the same time she was frightened. If Lord Burnham did break into the house, he might try to kill Peter before they were even aware that he was in the house.

The Marquis buttoned up his robe and then went to the chest of drawers.

Athina saw that on the top of it there was lying both a rifle and a revolver.

The Marquis picked up the revolver first and held it out to her.

"Carry this," he said, "and be very careful. It is loaded."

He then picked up the rifle and turned to Athina,

"I was thinking before I fell asleep that, although it is difficult to believe it, Burnham undoubtedly has someone in this house who is an informer. Somebody who must have told him where we were going today."

Athina looked startled.

"Do – you mean – a spy?" she questioned.

"It may be some half-witted scullion or an odd-job man who will accept money, having no idea of the consequences of what he might be doing."

The Marquis almost snapped the words at her.

Then, picking up the rifle, he walked towards the door.

"Peter is in my bed," she informed him.

"I have no wish for the boy to be frightened," the Marquis replied. "What we have to find out now is where Burnham intends to enter the house."

He did not say anything more but then opened the door into the corridor.

Athina followed him and they walked along the corridor, but not towards the main staircase that led to the hall.

Instead they went to what she knew was a secondary staircase that was seldom used.

There was just enough light in the corridor and at the foot of the stairs for them to see their way.

They reached the ground floor and the Marquis went quickly to the first of the rooms facing onto the courtyard and opened the door.

For a moment Athina did not know what he was looking for.

Then as he shut the door and went on to the next, she understood.

When the Adam brothers had practically rebuilt the whole house in about 1760, they had put on a new facade.

It made Rock Park look extremely impressive and very beautiful.

The ground floor had tall Georgian windows rising from only a few feet above ground level.

In consequence for safety they had strong wooden shutters inside and these were closed at night by one of the footman.

The Marquis hurried from room to room.

Athina realised that what he was expecting to find was that Lord Burnham's accomplice had left the shutters open in one of the rooms.

In which case, if the window was not fastened, he had only to push it up and he could then enter the room without any difficulty.

The Marquis opened door after door.

Athina began to think that he was mistaken and Lord Burnham was planning to enter the house by some other means.

At last in a sitting room next to the library the Marquis found just what he was seeking.

As he opened the door, Athina could see at first glance a glimpse of shining glass and this meant that the shutters were open.

The Marquis went into the room.

When Athina followed him, he did not walk towards the window.

Instead he moved to one side and stood behind an armchair.

Now Athina could see that the window was already raised.

There was just room enough for a man to put his leg over the sill and climb in.

She was wondering who among the Marquis's staff could have behaved so treacherously and she hoped that it was not someone who had been at Rock Park for a long time.

She recognised that she must not speak or move.

She was aware that the Marquis was standing motionless with his rifle at the ready.

He was staring intently at the window, but there was no sound from outside.

Athina began to wonder if perhaps Lord Burnham had not in fact come down the drive as Peter had dreamed he had done.

Perhaps he had changed his mind and gone away.

As her eyes became more accustomed to the darkness, she could see the stars. The clouds were moving away from the moon and the night air coming into the room was cool.

Then there was a sound.

It was only very faint, but unmistakably a sound in the courtyard.

Athina strained her ears to hear what was going on and then the sound came again, this time a little louder.

She was aware that the Marquis had drawn in his breath.

Although he had not moved, she knew that he had heard, as she had, the sounds coming from outside.

Now they came nearer and nearer still.

Somebody was moving stealthily and with covered shoes over the gravel outside.

Before she had expected it, so that she almost gave out a scream, there was a large dark figure in front of the window.

It was undoubtedly Lord Burnham and he was wearing black and this seemed to make him appear even more menacing.

There was a hood of some sort pulled over his head.

She thought too, although she could not see it clearly, that he wore a mask.

Now Athina saw that he held something white in his hand.

He looked up at the window as if he was appraising it.

Then, putting the hand that held whatever it was that was white, he put his leg over the sill.

As he did so, there was a sudden ominous growl and then a sharp bark.

Flash then rushed from behind Athina towards the window.

She had had no idea that he had left Peter and followed her and the Marquis downstairs. So he must have left her bedroom when she did.

Now he was barking furiously at Lord Burnham.

He threw his leg back sharply, dropping inside the room whatever it was he carried.

He staggered for a second outside the window.

Then, as Flash stood up on the sill barking at him, Athina heard him hurrying away.

He was no longer treading softly as he went, but half-running, half- stumbling.

The Marquis ran quickly to the window and leant out, watching Lord Burnham make for the shrubbery.

Athina bent down to pick up what he had dropped.

It appeared, when she looked at it, to be a white linen face-towel.

Then she was aware that there was something thicker inside it.

As she bent her head to inspect it, she noticed a strange smell and, before she could understand what it meant, the Marquis ordered her in a low voice,

"Put it down! He has saturated it with chloroform. It would have rendered Peter unconscious, then I imagine he would have suffocated him with a pillow."

Athina gave a cry of horror.

She dropped the towel as the Marquis had told her to do and then she bent forward to look out of the window.

Lord Burnham was obviously finding it very difficult to go back to where he had left his horse.

There was a delay of several minutes before he rode out from the shrubbery and proceeded towards the bridge.

As he did so, Athina became suddenly aware that the Marquis had gone down on one knee.

He was aiming his rifle at Lord Burnham.

It flashed through her mind that it would be very dangerous for him to shoot Lord Burnham.

Although he was an intruder and disguised, he was his brother-in-law and it would undoubtedly cause a tremendous scandal.

The Marquis would be involved in a Court case and might even be convicted of manslaughter.

She wanted to beg him not to do it.

And yet, even as she parted her lips to speak, she found it just impossible to do so.

Lord Burnham had now reached the narrow bridge.

As he did so, the clouds that had obscured the moon moved away completely.

The moonlight shone dazzlingly on the lake.

It lit the ancient bridge and the man in dark clothing approaching it on horseback.

"Don't shoot!" Athina started to cry out.

Then to her surprise she realised that the Marquis was pointing the rifle not at Lord Burnham but at the bridge itself.

It had been built in Elizabethan times and was made of bricks that had mellowed with age like the house itself.

At each end of the bridge there stood a small statue and, with the passing of the years, they had become somewhat worn and battered.

Now it was difficult to tell what they had originally represented.

The Marquis's father had always refused to have them renewed or even repaired.

The Marquis was now aiming at the statue at the far end of the bridge and Athina was puzzled by what he was doing.

She was aware that on the parapet of the bridge itself there were a number of birds. There were ducks and moorhens perched there for the night.

She remembered vaguely having noticed them before when she looked out of the window.

Now, as Lord Burnham's horse stepped gingerly onto the bridge, the Marquis took careful aim.

He fired at the statue beyond where the birds were roosting.

The explosion and the shattering of the stone caused them to fly squawking with fear and resentment across the bridge and onto the bank on the other side of it.

The horse, frightened by the sudden sound and the movement of the birds, reared up.

Lord Burnham, who was very obviously somewhat insecure in the saddle, was thrown.

He landed on the parapet of the bridge where he lay sprawled for a few seconds.

Then, because he was clearly too heavy and too much fuddled with drink to save himself, he slipped slowly backwards into the lake.

The last that Athina saw of him before he disappeared were his polished riding boots shining in the moonlight.

His horse bolted into the Park, its stirrups jangling as it vanished amongst the trees.

Athina watched as if spellbound and unable to move or make any sound.

The Marquis put down his rifle and rose to his feet.

"That is the end," he declared with considerable satisfaction. "The water is very deep there and anyway he was in no condition to swim."

He spoke like a man who had found the answer to a problem that had threatened to defeat him.

It was then that Athina gave a gasp.

The horror of all that she had just witnessed made her feel as if she was going to faint.

Hardly knowing what she was doing, she then moved towards the Marquis.

As he then put his arms around her, she hid her face against his shoulder.

Without even realising that she was crying the tears were running down her cheeks.

The Marquis held her close against him.

Then he said,

"It's all right, my darling! It is now all over and thank God that Peter is safe."

Startled at the way that he had addressed her, Athina raised her head to look up at him.

The moonlight coming through the window shone in her eyes, still wide and terrified.

Tears glistened on her cheeks and for a moment the Marquis just looked down at her.

Then he bent his head and his lips found hers.

Athina could not believe that it was happening.

As the Marquis's mouth held hers captive, she felt as if the stars fell from the sky and moved into her breast.

The Marquis's kiss lasted for what seemed an Eternity before he said,

"This is what I have been looking for. This is love, my precious."

Then he was kissing her once again, kissing her demandingly and possessively until she was no longer herself but a part of him.

It was impossible to think and impossible to breathe.

At last the Marquis said in a strange deep voice that sounded a little unsteady,

"I love you! *I love you*, Athina, and I had no idea that I could feel as I do at this moment."

"Y-you – love me – you really – love me?" Athina whispered.

"I adore you and I worship you! You are everything I have always wanted and the reason why I had no wish to marry anyone was that I did not believe that anyone like you really existed in this world."

He kissed the tears away from her eyes before he asked her,

"Now tell me that you love me too."

"I did not – know what – love would be like," Athina sighed. "But now I know – that it is glorious and wonderful. And – how – could I not – love you?"

"You told me I was the last man in the world you would marry," the Marquis reminded her, "but you are going to marry me, my lovely one, because I cannot live without you."

"I-I thought I – hated you," Athina confessed, "because you had neglected Peter – but now I know how wonderfully clever and kind you are – and I love – you more – than I can ever say."

"And I love you," the Marquis asserted. "My darling, how could we imagine that we would find each other in such a strange fashion?"

She knew that he was thinking that, if she had not been obliged to stay at the Posting inn, they might never have met.

If she had not befriended Peter, who happened to be in the room that communicated with hers, she would not have known that he was the Marquis's nephew.

It all seemed like a weird and complicated puzzle. Yet Fate had brought two people together who had both loathed the idea of being married.

The thought passed through both their minds.

Then the Marquis asked,

"How soon will you marry me? I have no intention of waiting. I want you now, at once, and I am so desperately afraid of losing you, my darling one?"

"You will – never lose – me," Athina said, "and I will – marry you – whenever you wish."

The Marquis pulled her closer to him before he answered.

"I would marry you at this very moment if I could."

The bright moonlight shone on her face and he looked down at her lingeringly before he said,

"How can you be so utterly beautiful? But it is much more than that, you are everything I want in a woman, everything I dreamt a woman should be like. But I was convinced that she existed only in my imagination."

"I-I am so – afraid I might – disappoint you," Athina whispered. "I knew when I – came to your room – tonight and – saw you asleep that – you were not only the most – handsome man I have – ever seen but also too – marvellous to be human."

The Marquis laughed.

"I assure you, my darling, I am very human when I kiss you and want you to be mine. And we each recognise in the other something that is different."

He paused for a moment.

Then he said quietly,

"I believe God made us for each other and that is why our love is different from what it would ever be with anybody else."

"How can you – say such – marvellous things – to me?" Athina asked. "Things I have – thought in my heart – but never – imagined a man would ever – say them to me."

The Marquis drew in his breath.

"We have a great deal to learn about each other," he said, "and therefore the sooner we are married the better."

Athina moved a little closer to him.

"Could we," she asked hesitatingly, "just be – married here in the country? Either in the village Church where I was – baptised – or perhaps in your private Chapel, which I have not yet seen – although I know that you must have one."

"Would that make you happy?" the Marquis asked.

"I would be happy – anywhere with you," Athina answered, "but I am afraid that what we feel now is just – part of the – moonlight and a wonderful – wonderful dream."

She hid her face against his neck again as she added,

"I have lived quietly in the – country and – know nothing – of London. I am– afraid of your – smart friends. If they – laughed or sniggered – it would – spoil what we are – feeling for each other now."

She spoke so softly that the Marquis could hardly hear what she was saying.

Then his arms tightened around her and he said,

"You are quite right and that is what I feel myself. We will be married here in my private Chapel by my Chaplain, who is also the Vicar of the Parish."

He smiled at her before he went on,

"And the only witnesses to our Wedding will be Peter and Mrs. Beckwith."

"Peter will be so thrilled," Athina enthused.

Then she gave a little exclamation.

"Oh, Denzil, is it true – really – true that we need no longer be – afraid for – him? I know it is – only a matter of days – but I feel we have been – fighting for him for – years. Because you are the Knight of Chivalry who I thought existed only in books, is he now – safe and need never be – afraid again?"

She felt as if the words tumbled from her mouth and she had no control over them.

The Marquis did not answer.

He merely kissed her until once again they were flying past the stars and no longer on earth.

He knew that it had been a very long search to find a woman who could take his mother's place at Rock Park.

Athina filled the shrine in his heart that he had hesitated to admit was there, even to himself.

He had found her.

She was young, unspoilt and very innocent.

Their love, he knew, was ageless and came from Eternity and would go on to Eternity.

It was the glory and wonder that he had been sure he would never find however hard he looked.

"*This is love,*" he repeated again as he carried Athina up into the sky.

OTHER BOOKS IN THIS SERIES

The Barbara Cartland Eternal Collection is the unique opportunity to collect all five hundred of the timeless beautiful romantic novels written by the world's most celebrated and enduring romantic author.

Named the Eternal Collection because Barbara's inspiring stories of pure love, just the same as love itself, the books will be published on the internet at the rate of four titles per month until all five hundred are available.

The Eternal Collection, classic pure romance available worldwide for all time.